NEVER CAN SAY GOODBYE

ABOUT THE AUTHOR

Judi Lewinson is the namesake behind the boutique entertainment firm, Judi Lewinson Media, LLC, which specializes in the development and production of film, television, web, radio, literary and special event titles.

When she is not writing, Judi loves playing basketball & dj'ing.

Keep up to date with Judi Lewinson's releases:

Website: www.judilew.com
Facebook: facebook.com/judilew
Twitter: twitter.com/judilew
SMS: Text **judilew** to **721669**

WWW.JUDILEW.COM

To Agent Kiki, the LS Family

and the sisters of SBU.

Thank-you.

"A woman never forgets the men she could have had; a man, the woman he couldn't"

-Anon-

CHAPTER ONE

The hills are alive in Los Angeles. The sun whispers its mid-evening valediction as it seeks its final resting place beyond the cooling waters of the baronial Pacific Ocean. A breath beyond Hollywood, the 101 North Freeway plays host to the few scattered, overworked and underpaid commuters trudging their way home. It was unusually warm for this late in September. The perilous fires in the hills have finally died down, but the cautionary tale of smoking in the hills plays over the airways of the evening news.

Several homes have been lost and the many families displaced are the headlines in this evenings report. The smoldering effects of a careless hiker lay faint in the distance. Truth is, the hills aren't the only things that are smoking this evening.

As Southern Californians resign indoors for their eventide rituals of dinner, drinks and relaxation, an affluent and extremely amorous young couple have set aside their romantic dinner in favor of a more salacious dessert. Smooth jazz from the satellite radio station provides the sensual soundtrack to their carnal desires.

Their passion flows sovereign as the young man crashes his lover against the living room wall, inches from the unlit fireplace. It's so hot that a cool breath of air would never survive passage between them. Had they been in public their brash and unbridled osculation would have more than satisfied the gloss of what is crude.

Fingers interlaced. Explicit kisses. Bodies pressed together their passions rise. He wants her. She *needs* him. It's been far too long for both of them. The amatory duel for sexual dominance only serves to excite the young couple even further as they kiss, constantly exchanging positions. Him against the wall. Her against the wall. Him. Her. Him. Her. Him.

Exasperatedly, she pushes him away.

He stumbles backwards and lands on the nearby chesterfield. Both are breathless – so naughty, but oh so nice. They are the beautiful people…and they know it.

She giggles at his awkward positioning and teases him with a sly and sexy swish of her narrow waist and voluptuous hips. He emits a low prurient growl, raises his eyebrows and motions for her to come closer. Feeling mischievously wicked she shakes her head with a shameless smile, teases him with her swarthy tresses and motions for him to follow her instead. Laughter fills the air as she takes off, just past his reach, up the main stairs.

Eagerly, he gives into this wanton chase. In his haste, the young man accidently knocks over a picture frame. It's a wedding photo; the happy couple on their most fabulous day.

Interesting...the woman next to him in the photograph is NOT the woman he's chasing up those stairs.

CHAPTER TWO

Moments later, the door to the master bedroom hangs slightly ajar, as if giving permission for a naughty peep into the erotic escapades of the young, the rich and the restless.

Clothes are strewn from the doorway all the way to the oversized custom framed bed. This mix of his and hers serves as a prelude to the insatiable acts of passion that fill the room. The oversized chest mirror holds the clouded reflection of the young couple's lovemaking. At times he guides their passion to a primitive and demanding position before bandying to a more sensuously urbane and tantric exchange.

They pause, holding each other's gaze. In this moment a million words are said, though not a syllable is uttered. He has much to give her and she is more than ready to receive. She draws her breath short as he lowers his head between her thighs.

Bliss.

CHAPTER THREE

If one listens carefully the muffled moans of a requited romance can be heard coming from upstairs. Downstairs the stereo continues to play commercial free smooth jazz and soul fusion, but just beyond that can be heard the subtle rustling of the front door's deadbolt.

A beat passes.

Success.

The lock turns and the front door slowly opens, granting the stranger entry into the home. The sun is no longer on hand to cast an amiable light into the already dim foyer. The stranger enters and quietly closes the door with a gloved hand.

Passing through towards the living room the stranger pauses at the bottom of the main staircase as if listening for a moment before moving on. The living room, while disturbed, is not in shambles. The stranger moves through at a curious pace.

Looking towards the dining room the stranger sees one of the two place settings. From this vantage point the second setting isn't visible. The stranger continues to move through the living room and pauses to pick up the fallen wedding photo. There is a slight irritation at the casual nature upon which it was cast upon the floor. The stranger looks at the happy couple one time before carefully restoring the frame to its rightful place and position.

Upstairs, the young couple is fully engaged in their favorite karma sutra positions. He can't get enough of her. She moans with pleasure and pulls him closer. He kisses her slowly as their shakras unify entrusting their passions to the will of the moment. She surrenders herself to his hypnotic rhythm. He is only more than happy to oblige her proliferating passions.

Both are oblivious to the daunting verity that they are no longer alone in the house.

CHAPTER FOUR

The stranger is moving silently up the stairs now. The sounds of lovemaking grows increasingly louder with each step the stranger takes. Quietly passing by the other rooms without pause the stranger gingerly heads towards the master bedroom. At first the strangers pace seems to quicken, but then dramatically slows upon drawing closer to the bedroom door.

Carson Winters is in the throes of passions with his girlfriend of the last three months, Franchesca Devaux. Theirs is a love affair that harbors no sensual demarcations, but requires the utmost of social discretion. At first it was strenuous, but the rules surrounding their romance soon turned into an unspoken aphrodisiac. These bedroom walls often serve as the proverbial sidelines to their pitch of salacious copulation…until now…

Neither Carson nor Franchesca are aware that they are being watched…

…BY THE BRIDE IN THE PICTURE!!!

\

CHAPTER FIVE

A bristling rage is building at the doorway to the Winters' master bedroom as Marissa Winters tries not to be overcome by the shock of the erotic scene that is playing out before her.

Slowly, Marissa pushes open the door to her bedroom and quietly approaches her traitorous husband and the woman she thought was her best friend as they fornicate without regard for her, before her.

She manages only a few paces into the room before Franchesca sees her.

"Ohmigod! Marissa!"

"Huh?"

Oblivious to the sudden change of dynamics, Carson looks over and is visibly stunned to see his eerily calm wife standing only a few paces away from them.

Now is a good time to panic...

"Marissa, baby…" he stumbles. "I…"

It doesn't matter what Carson is about to say next. Marissa doesn't stick around long enough for her husband to finish. Horrified, she takes off out of the bedroom leaving the betrayers of trust behind in a twist of satin sheets and shame.

"Marissa!" Carson calls out after her.

He fumbles to get out of the bed and searches for his boxer shorts. He looks at Franchesca surprised that she is hasn't moved.

"Well, don't just sit there!" he barks, "Get dressed!"

What he doesn't realize is that Franchesca is caught in a state of paralyzing panic. This was not supposed to have happened and even when she had played back the potential scenario of a moment like this, this was *not* what happened. From the very first time they had kissed both of them knew it was wrong.

Now they are caught.

The sound of the front door slamming is heard just as Carson locates his pants. Rushing, trying to step into them and chase after his wife at the same time, he falls flat on his face.

"Dammit!" he curses.

Franchesca snaps out of her fugue state and starts to get dressed. She moves around the room at a more stoic pace, locating her clothing and painstakingly putting them back on.

Her panic has turned inward.

"She didn't even say a word, Carson," she says quietly. "She didn't say a word."

Carson has managed to get his pants on. He runs out the bedroom without a reply, more alarmed by his wife's insouciance. Both of them know it's not in Marissa's nature to just shut down and walk away. What they had just witnessed was a whole new level of rage.

Carson slips on a few steps as he rushes down the stairs, but catches himself mid-fall. He desperately flings the front door open just in time to see the taillights of his wife's SL 500 peeling out of their driveway and into the street.

"Marissa!" he calls out. "Marissa, come back!"

Carson's cries are to no avail. Marissa's Mercedes disappears in the distance leaving Carson alone in the doorway. Cursing under his breath, he closes the door in defeat. Overwhelmed by the wave of mottled emotions he sits heavily at the foot of the main staircase and collapses his head in his hands. A colossal truth has violently interjected its existence into their selfish lie.

A few moments later Franchesca comes down the stairs and gingerly steps past Carson.

"I've called a cab," she says quietly. "It should be here in ten minutes."

Carson slowly lifts his head and stares blankly past her.

"She's gone," he says completely dejected. "She…she just left…"

CHAPTER SIX

Franchesca's mind races as her panic continues to set in. She keeps checking at the window for the cab she has hired.

Her mind is racing as panic really begins to set in. This was not the way that things were supposed to happen. As she paces the foyer now, Franchesca can't figure out how they'd gotten here. There was no blaming her friend for being upset, but Marissa's reaction was all wrong.

In all the years that Franchesca has known Marissa this is not the type of response that she would have ever expected. The truth is after seeing the look of rage in Marissa's eyes all Franchesca can envision is her life coming to some violent TMZ splashed end before the dawn. No one ever just walks away from these things. Franchesca had to get out of there.

"I thought you said she was going to be away until tomorrow, Carson," she starts to ramble. "We have to fix this. You've got to call her. I mean, she didn't even say a word."

Carson remains despondent and unresponsive as Franchesca blathers on about how wrong everything is and what are they going do now. Her voice drones on endlessly like an army of vuvuzelas at a World Cup final. Carson is so zoned out now that he can barely understand a thing she's saying.

Finally, Franchesca stops talking and just stares out the window.

Time ticks on. Neither of them speaks. The silence and shame grows increasingly deafening. Here come the vuvuzelas again. This was never supposed to have happened. The three of them have been friends for years. Franchesca was Marissa's maid of honour. Marissa had been there for Franchesca in college when her parents had unexpectedly been killed in a plane crash. Best friends for life, is what they'd said. Now everything has changed.

"She didn't say anything," Carson finally sighs with an absent stare.

"I *just* said that…Hey!"

Franchesca snaps her fingers repeatedly in Carson's face.

"Snap out of it!" she yells. "Don't you see what has happened, Carson? We are so busted, right now. What are we going to do?"

Carson looks at her in annoyance.

"Shut up."

His voice is low and deathly even.

"I wouldn't be surprised if…"

"Shut up."

Through clenched teeth Carson's voice grows louder; a controlled rage as Franchesca prattles on.

"I wouldn't be surprised if -"

"Shut… Up…"

He can feel his chest tightening and the walls closing in. His temperature is rising.

"She went ahead and got a -"

Finding it difficult to breathe, Carson's frustration can no longer be contained.

"I said, SHUT UP!!!"

Franchesca is startled by the sudden outburst.

"Hey!" she retorts. "I'm in this too you know. I'm supposed to be her best friend."

Without a further word, Carson gets up and heads back upstairs. Aggravated and confused, Franchesca quickly follows suit, annoyingly on his heels the entire way.

"Where are you going?" she asks.

"I've got to call her," he replies without turning around.

"What are you going to say?" There is a panic in her voice.

"I don't know."

"Where do you think she went?"

"I don't know."

"Well, do you think she'll come back?"

Carson stops walking and abruptly turns to face Franchesca in a rage, causing her to nearly stumble backwards.

"I said, I *do not* know, Frankie!" he screams. "I don't know! I don't know! I DON'T KNOW!!!"

They were back in the bedroom; the scene of the crime.

A heavy silence falls again. How many times had they been here? How many times had they said that this was the last time?

How many times?

CHAPTER SEVEN

"It's ringing."

Carson sits on the edge of his bed with his mobile phone at his ear. Franchesca waits anxiously. At first she takes a seat next to Carson on the bed but quickly rises, seeing as this is the source of their current predicament. As she stands she overhears Marissa's outgoing message on her voicemail.

Carson curses under his breath, waiting for the beep.

"Marissa! Marissa, it's me…Baby, I'm sorry," his voice is full of desperation. "Please… I never meant for this to happen… I mean…"

Carson pauses in an effort to find some semblance of composure. He's not used to being in this position. As a major executive in the music business he was used to people seeking out his favor. Carson Winters could move millions of dollars without even batting an eye. This moment right now was proving to be his most difficult undertaking. Humble-pie has never been a dish he's ever had to order.

Carson takes a deep breath before continuing.

"Marissa," he says slowly. "Babe, please call me. I'm so sorry."

He hangs up the phone and turns to face Franchesca. His eyes are hopeful that his apology will not be rebuffed.

"You didn't tell her that you love her," Franchesca says.

"Yeah, I did."

Franchesca shakes her head to the contrary. Carson thinks back and quickly realizes that she is right.

He picks up the phone and dials Marissa again.

CHAPTER EIGHT

Marissa has been driving for more than some time now. It's late and the road is mostly empty, but for a few cars in the restaurant district.

Her mobile phone sits on the seat next to her ringing yet again. The call display indicates that it's her husband. Once again she'll let the machine take his call. Too much has happened. She's not ready to deal.

Silent tears begin to fall as Marissa drives westward along Ventura Boulevard.

Within moments her tears are soon flowing like a river as she drives faster and faster.

The phone rings again. Marissa lets the call go to voicemail. This is the seventh missed call.

Her radio isn't on, but the sound of any Toni Braxton's melodies of heartbreak echoes loudly in her mind, leading Melissa to sob openly as she blindly whips through intersection after intersection.

As the Mercedes pick up speed, Marissa is no longer on the favorable side of the green light. With each light turning to amber as she speeds through the intersections Marissa is oblivious to her changing fate.

Heading west, well past Sepulveda Marissa doesn't even see the red light and enters the next major intersection at extraordinary speeds. A lone cross traffic

Range Rover driver blasts the horn and swerves to avoid hitting Marissa. There is only a frame of chance between a safe passage and tragedy. Marissa is violently jarred back into the moment as the luxury SUV narrowly misses the back end of the Mercedes.

"Bloody hell, M," she scolds herself, "Focus."

Marissa swerves again to avoid the accident as well and slams on the brakes when she clears the intersection. Her car fishtails into a dangerous spin. Marissa screams, but manages to turn into the spin and stop the car, just before t-boning a parked Lexus on the side of the road.

In the midst of her panic she fails to sink the clutch and her car stalls out upon stopping. The Range Rover is long gone. Marissa can barely breathe.

The stress of it all is far too overwhelming for her. Sobbing, uncontrollably, it dawns on Marissa that she almost died just now. This truly is the worst day of her life.

Marissa collapses her forehead against the top of her steering wheel and continues to sob profusely.

This is not supposed to be her life.

CHAPTER NINE

It had taken all evening and most of the night but finally the house was clean. All evidence of his earlier affair has been removed. Only the stereo was playing now. The volume, like the overall mood of the house, is low.

Carson is seated in the living room of his house. A single lamp shines in the corner, but he is not concerned about the room's lack of lighting. For him it's about his home's lack of love…and he knows this moment is his fault.

He has been calling Marissa all evening without any response. It's after midnight. Carson is beginning to worry.

Suddenly his phone rings.

Startled Carson almost drops his mobile when he reaches to answer it.

"Hello! Marissa? Baby is that you?"

"No, it's me."

Franchesca.

Carson makes no attempt to mask his disappointment.

"Oh, hey," he says.

She doesn't play hurt by his lack of enthusiasm. Those were the games of yesterday. Now, a more pressing matter was at hand.

"Has she called?"

"No."

Franchesca is in casual sleepwear, curled up on her couch. The television is on mute as she surfs and talks on the phone. There isn't anything interesting on. Even if there was, the current situation precluded either of them from focusing on anything else.

"She hasn't called me back either," she says quietly. "I've been calling all night."

"Me too," Carson replies, "Where do you think she went?"

"Honestly, I don't know."

Franchesca turns off the television and begins to straighten up a few things in her apartment's living room before grabbing her glass of wine and moving to her bedroom.

"Whenever you two have ever had a fight before," she continues, "Mar would come and see me. Clearly, that's not the case this time around."

"Maybe she went to the office?"

His voice is hopefully.

Franchesca sips her wine before answering.

"Nope, I called there," she says. "Security said they hadn't seen her all night."

Carson uses the remote to turn off the stereo and turn on the television. He flips through the channels oblivious to the silence between them.

"Carson?"

He waits a moment before answering. His voice is barely audible when he does.

"Yeah?" he says; his voice is sad.

"You know how we've been saying that Mar's been different lately? Distant, depressed..."

Carson sits up. He doesn't like where this is going.

"Uh-huh."

He turns the television off, tosses the remote onto the couch and makes his way upstairs.

Franchesca is in bed as they continue to talk. How many nights had they shared like this? Well, not exactly like this...

There is a worried tone in her voice as she adjusts her pillows.

"She didn't flip out, Carson," she says. "I'm worried. Marissa never, ever just plays it cool... It's like she just resigned."

"I know," he replies. "I'm worried too."

Both of them know that there is no escaping the seriousness of the situation. No one ever means for anyone to get hurt, but in the end when selfishness is involved someone always does. The only questions now are, how deep is the pain and is the any hope of finding healing?

Franchesca swallows hard. She must measure her words. Still, there is no easy to say what she says next.

"Well, I was thinking," she says, "Well, what if... I mean, you don't think she would..."

She pauses, perhaps a moment too long.

"...hurt herself?" she finally says.

Carson sits upright in his bed, alarmed.

"What???" he protests, "Oh, hell nah! Mar ain't even like that."

Carson's next few words are said more to convince himself than Franchesca.

"She's coming back…she coming back," he says. "And when she does, I'll be right here waiting for her."

CHAPTER TEN

After sobbing until she can't sob anymore Marissa finally raises her head from the steering wheel. Amazingly, well not really for LA, although her car is positioned cross-lane no one has stopped to see there has been an accident or if she is okay. It is in this moment that her greatest anxiety becomes her loudest truth.

She is truly alone.

So many questions race through her mind. How did she get here? Why would they do this to her? How could they disrespect the vows of marriage like this? The three of them had been friends since college. Didn't that mean anything? How long had this been going on?

Never in a million years did Marissa Winters ever think that this would be her life.

Marissa sighs and resigns to the fact that her marriage is not what she thought it was. Her heart may be broken, but she couldn't just sit here.

"Alright, M," she says to herself in a heavy sigh. "Now what?"

Marissa fumbles with the ignition and starts her car again. At first she turns around to head home but quickly changes her mind and turns the car around again continuing west on Ventura. She's nearing Woodland Hills.

Marissa passes through the sleeping town until she arrives at Version, a small jazz lounge just off of the strip. The parking lot is sparse, but the vehicles on hand make it clear that this is where money comes to chill. Marissa parks her car, takes a deep breath, slowly exhales and steps out.

The walk across the parking lot provides Marissa with a few moments to regain her composure. Upon crossing the threshold of the lounge Marissa feels a sense of salutation. The sound of the live band inside and the incredible female vocalist who leads them is already making her feel a little better.

CHAPTER ELEVEN

The jazz lounge, dim yet comfortingly lit, holds a deep red lived in sentient. The cool brick that makes up the back wall, mixture of jazz greats and Bua paintings, single-lit tabletop candles and the faint scent of Jamaican Spice incense instantly transport patrons from this affluent west coast town to a space in time akin to an east coast soulful speakeasy.

There are a select number of patrons dotted about this soothing space. Some tables hold couples while others lay vacant. The band plays a mixture of jazz interpreted hip hop covers as well as soul classics and original numbers.

Marissa passes through the main area of the lounge and easily maneuvers her way to the bar. There are a few other patrons, mostly male, seated at the far end of the bar. Wanting to be alone she sidles up to the more vacant area and takes a stool. There's only one bartender on staff this evening. He glances over at Marissa and smiles as he retrieves another beer from the fridge. His chiseled good looks, subtle confidence and apparent charm, as he slides a Red Stripe to another patron are proof positive that every bill in his tips jar is worth it.

"You enjoy that, Jimmy," he says with a smile.

The bartender casually walks over to where Marissa is seated, melancholy, watching the band. She nods in time to their music. This is exactly what she needed to take her mind off of life at home.

The band is nearing the end of a boss translation and hip hop infused interpretation of Billy Holiday's "Lady Sings the Blues".

"Welcome to Version," the bartender says. "What can I get you?"

Marissa turns to look at him. She's aware of his good looks but doesn't stumble over them; her voice akin to her spirit is heavy-laden as she speaks.

"Goose and Seven, please," she says.

The bartender nods. Like any good bartender he knows that there is a story here. It's only a matter of time before he hears it.

He smiles to put her at ease.

"One Grey Goose and Seven coming up."

Without a word, Marissa returns her attention to the performance on stage. It's a classic Ella & Duke number, "Learnin' The Blues". Marissa manages a reflective smile as the tune plays.

Moments later, the bartender returns with Marissa's drink. A subtle half-smile plays upon her lips as she accepts the much needed libation.

"A smile," he says. "That's nice."

"Thank you."

Marissa reaches for her purse to pay, but the bartender waves her off.

"First drink is on the house…on me."

She smiles again; fuller this time.

"Thank you," she says.

"Sebastian."

Marissa pauses for a moment. Of course he is.

"Sebastian, right," she says. "Thank you, Sebastian."

Marissa takes a sip on her beverage and smiles. It's perfect.

"You're welcome…"

He waits. She appreciates the subtle flirtation.

"Marissa," she finally says.

"Marissa," Sebastian says restfully in an effort to commit her name to memory. "Well, thank you for the smile. I just hope whoever he is gets his act together soon."

Sensing her confusion he continues.

"In my line of work you come to recognize these things. Cheers."

Sebastian walks away to help another customer before Marissa can answer. She looks after him in slight wonderment before retrieving her drink and reclining to a lone table by the side of the stage.

Her purse is vibrating.

Marissa opens it and takes out her mobile phone. Checking the caller ID she sees that yet again her husband is calling. Marissa turns off her phone and tosses it back inside her purse.

The action does not go unnoticed by Sebastian as he serves another patron. He nods to himself, knowingly.

This is a story all too familiar in this town.

CHAPTER TWELVE

The band is playing their final set. It's nearly 2 am and Marissa is at her table feeling pretty good. The four empty glasses serve as evidence to her jovial condition. She is nursing her fifth vodka seven when Sebastian comes over.

"Hey, Sebastian," she slightly slurs, "I think we'll have another."

Sebastian starts to clear the empties.

"I think we're done," he replies.

Sebastian smiles and taps his watch.

"Last call was twenty minutes ago," he says.

He looks in the direction of an empty chair. Marissa shrugs, not bothered either way so Sebastian takes a seat.

"You know, I get the feeling that whatever pain you're trying to drink away is only going to be there to greet you in the morning," he says empathetically. "Besides, I don't want you cussing me out because you've got to nurse that AND a hangover."

Marissa sets her glass down and pushes it away with a half smile.

"Aah, there's that smile again," Sebastian says. "I like it."

"You think you got me all figured out, don't you?" Marissa says sitting up. "Hmm? Good looking cat in a smooth ass spot, servin' up drinks in your-"

She pauses to look him up and down. She can't deny to herself that he looks more than just good.

"What are those? Coogi Jeans and a French Connection tee?" she continues. "Figure you know a little somethin', huh?"

"I appreciate the uh, compliment," he replies, "but I didn't say all that."

Sebastian knows that the hint of an attitude has nothing to do with him. He looks around the room as the band breaks into its final number. But for a few regulars most of the customers are gone.

Marissa is tempted to cover her mood with another sip of her drink. She reaches for her glass and then changing her mind plays with the promo card on the table instead.

Sebastian returns his focus to her. He leans in closer.

"Come dance with me," he says gently.

"Excuse me?"

"Dance with me."

This time his voice is firmer. Marissa begins to protest, but Sebastian takes her hand and in one fluid movement she is on her feet.

"Come on," he says. "It's the last song. Besides, I gotta feeling…"

He leads the few paces it takes to get to the dance floor.

"And what feeling is that?" she asks.

He pulls her close into their slow dance and whispers, "That you deserve better than the day you've had."

Though the tears are on standby, Marissa doesn't want to cry. She allows herself to be drawn closer as Sebastian leads. His embrace is full of confidence. His silent strength bolsters her waning resolve. In this moment "Sentimental Mood" is more than just a song.

Marissa closes her eyes as they dance and after a few moments, gently rests her head on Sebastian's shoulder. He hugs her and they continue dancing.

A single silent tear runs down Marissa's cheek.

This moment, right here, right now is exactly what she needs.

Sebastian smiles when finally... *finally* a more relaxed Marissa slowly exhales. She feels safe here.

If anyone had been watching them more closely they would have sworn that in that very moment they'd seen a glint of suspicious intentions flash across Sebastian eyes.

Just as quickly, Sebastian relaxes his gaze, looks down at Marissa and smiles.

CHAPTER THIRTEEN

The clock on the wall says it's nearly 3 a.m. All of the Version patrons have long since gone home. The band has broken down their setup and is heading out of the lounge.

Marissa and Sebastian are at the bar. He's wiping the surface down while she pushes the remaining nuts in a nearby bowl around with a straw.

Sebastian comes over and looks at her, the bowl and then back at her.

"You gonna eat those?"

"Not if my life depended on it," replies matter-of-factly.

Sebastian chuckles to himself and takes the bowl from her.

"What? It's unsanitary," she says. "I saw this thing on Oprah…"

"You're drunk."

"Am not."

He leans in.

"Deny it all you want," he teases, "but in my *professional* opinion you *my dear*… are most definitely…drizzunk."

Marissa giggles.

"There's that smile again… You could kill a man with that smile," he says.

Suddenly, a violent flash of Carson and Franchesca in her bed crashes through

Marissa's mind causing her smile to quickly fade. She looks away as tears begin to fall.

"Hey, hey…"

Sebastian gently lifts and turns her chin to look at him. His eyes search her face in hopes of understanding.

"What happened?" he asks. "What did I say?"

Embarrassed, Marissa wipes away her tears and looks at Sebastian apologetically.

"I'm sorry. It's not you," she replies. "You didn't say anything wrong… You've been… perfect."

Suddenly feeling a little self-conscious, Sebastian resumes wiping down the counter space in from of them. He looks up at her, differently this time. Marissa holds his gaze. For a moment it seems like they are the only two people in the world and then the moment is gone.

Sebastian clears his throat and starts cleaning again.

"So what happened today?" he asks.

"Strangest thing," Marissa replies and looks off into the distance. "I came home."

Sebastian is finished cleaning.

"I don't get it," he says.

"Have you ever felt like you're losing yourself? I mean, I'm in this relationship...for better or for worse, right? But, I can't help but to feel like I'm shrinking inside myself sometimes," she says. "So, on this trip I threw myself into my work. I figured Carson and I could try again when I got back."

"Try again?"

Marissa takes a moment before continuing.

"We were trying to have a baby," she says quietly. "Our schedules got crazy. *Bad* crazy. We barely saw each other and when we did… there was this… this pressure…"

"So what happened?"

"Strange enough, I'm hundreds of miles away in the middle of a business presentation when it suddenly hits me," she says. "I missed my husband. I missed that man. I craved him. So, when things wrapped up earlier than expected I got on the first flight home."

Sebastian smiles.

"You had to get to your man."

Marissa pauses. Her eyes are sad again. He sees the change, but rather than speaking Sebastian waits. Right now, it's his job to just listen.

"I was right wicked in my presentation," Marissa continues, regaining her composure. "Spot on. Nothing left now but for legal to push the paperwork. Everyone wanted to go out and have a few drinks to celebrate; maybe do some sightseeing in the morning and catch our regular flight the next night."

Marissa laughs to herself at her ignorance.

"Not me though," she continues. "I'm *so* stupid. Me! I wanted to go home... Home to my... *husband*."

Sebastian comes from behind the bar and takes a seat on the stool next to Marissa. She wipes angrily wipes away a tear that falls as she continues her story.

"I was so excited," she says. "I hadn't seen him in a week. Closing this account meant a huge bonus. A guaranteed promotion, corner office... I even negotiated to get more time off. No more travelling every other week. The works."

She pauses to look at Sebastian, her eyes pleading for some sign of understanding. She adjusts her wedding band. Suddenly it feels more like a noose around her finger.

"I just wanted to celebrate with the man who had always been in my corner. Pushing me..." she sighs. "To go after the big prize. Hmmph."

"Pushing me away, more like it," she continues. "He said he didn't mind that I was away so much."

Sebastian places his hand on Marissa's, never taking his eyes off of her.

"He said he knew it was only temporary."

"So what happened?" he asks.

"Like I said, I came home," Marissa says. She looks at her wedding band and then back at Sebastian. It's really starting to feel tight.

"There were candles lit…" she says. "I could smell dinner as soon as I came in…"

"Someone gave him the heads up?"

"That's what I thought! When I came in I expected him to be in the living room, glass of wine, watching television, waiting for me… I hoped, but he wasn't there."

Marissa's cadence was far more measured as images of what happened next crossed her mind.

"So," she says, "I went upstairs… and… I heard sounds… coming…"

She begins to break down into tears.

"Coming from our bedroom," she cries. "I walked into the room and I couldn't believe what I was seeing. I mean, my husband and my BEST friend having a righteous shag! IN OUR BED!!!"

There is no stopping her tears now. Sebastian pulls Marissa into a hug and holds her as she cries.

"Hey, hey there," he says, kissing her forehead. "It's not your fault, Marissa. It's not your fault."

An ominous glint passes over his eyes. He knows that he's got her.

CHAPTER FOURTEEN

Carson has fallen asleep in the chair the master bedroom while watching the television. It's nearly 4:30 in the morning. A loud commercial jolts him from his sleep. It takes him a moment to get his bearings. Looking around the room his eyes stop on the bed.

No Marissa.

CHAPTER FIFTEEN

"Thank you, Sebastian. I really needed this," Marissa says with a sweet smile.

Both she and Sebastian are outside Version lounge beside Marissa's car. There's a slight chill in the air. Sebastian is happy to see her smiling again as they exchange a jovial moment.

It's clear that neither of them really wants this night to end. Sebastian's posture shifts and he casually on purpose brushes the tuck of her jacket; a slight yet effective flirtation.

It's now or never.

"Look," he says in a cool tone. "You've been drinking and even though some time has passed since the last glass, I don't think you should drive home."

There's a hint of something more in his voice. Marissa looks up at Sebastian. The street lamp handsomely catches his chiseled profile. She knows that they're on dangerous ground. Reflective, she looks away.

"I can't go home," she agrees. She nervously bites at her knuckle. "He's only going to be there waiting for me."

"I'd offer you a night at my place, but my house is getting renovated," he replies. He subtly licks his lips as he continues. "Best I can do is to get you a room at my buddy's hotel… Comp'd of course."

Marissa smiles at the gesture. Maybe she should go home. The way Sebastian looks in the moonlight Marissa is tempted to stay and have a night of revenge on her husband. As if sensing her forbidden thoughts, Sebastian cocks his head to the side, leans closer and smiles.

"What do you say, Marissa?" he asks insidiously. "What do you want to do tonight?"

CHAPTER SIXTEEN

The sound of a man singing from within the shower gently stirs a peacefully sleeping Marissa. Sleepily she rubs her eyes, slowly sits up and looks around. The sheets are pulled back on one side while she lay bundled nicely on the other. It takes her a moment to gather her bearings. Seeing Sebastian's shirt and the sound of the shower turning off brings Marissa to a very sobering realization. Clearly, she was not the only one to spend the night in her bed.

The bathroom door opens just as a panicked Marissa is about to "check" beneath the sheets. Sebastian emerges barefoot and shirtless in jeans.

He looks really, really good and now Marissa is even more worried. He smiles.

"Don't worry," he says. "We didn't do anything."

"I… We…" she stammers.

"Were on our best behavior," he finishes.

Marissa lets out a quiet sigh of relief although she has to admit, watching him now reading the menu, that she wasn't quite certain she'd be sorry if they hadn't been.

Sensing her eyes on him, Sebastian looks up and passes her the menu.

"I'll buy you breakfast and then let you get home to your husband."

CHAPTER SEVENTEEN

There is no calming Carson Winters this morning. He's late for work, his wife hasn't come home, and he's pacing his kitchen floor frantically while trying to fix his coffee.

"No!" he's shouting into the phone. "What I'm saying is that she DIDN'T COME HOME LAST NIGHT!"

Carson is clearly having a break from reality as his anxiety approaches critical mass. His best friend and business partner, Jacob

Plum is trying his best to keep Carson calm, but it appears to be to no avail.

"What am I supposed to do?" Carson continues. "My wife is pissed and didn't come home, dude! Mar ain't like that! Never go to bed mad… Those are the rules!"

"Yeah man, but you threw the rules out when you dipped out."

"You don't think I know that? It wasn't supposed to be like this."

Carson takes a frustrated sip of his coffee but it's too hot. He curses silently to himself.

There's a noise. A lock turning.

Carson stops pacing as he hears the front door open. He sets his mug down and walks out into the leaving room.

Marissa is home.

"Yo, J, gotta go, " he says into the phone. "She just walked in... I'll see you at the studio."

Carson hangs up the phone. Marissa stands silent. Her luggage is at the foot of the stairs... for now.

It seems like an eternity is passing by as they face one another.

"Baby, where were you?" Carson finally says rushing over to hug his wife. She stiffens in his embrace.

"I was calling you all night. Didn't you get any of my messages?" He yammers. "I was so worried. I didn't know what to think."

Carson steps back awaiting an answer. His wife gives him a deathly cold look before speaking.

"Funny, you didn't seem so worried about where I was when you were shagging my best friend," she retorts, her tone drips equally with ice. "Student becomes the teacher."

Marissa pushes past Carson and heads into the kitchen.

"Marissa," he calls after her.

No answer.

Carson takes a deep breath and follows her.

"Marissa," he says. "Marissa!"

Marissa abruptly turns to face her husband, causing him to stumble backwards.

"What!"

Carson knew it wasn't going to be easy to talk with his wife, but this is a whole other level of rage. Still, this is their marriage on the line and they need to talk.

"I was worried about you," he says.

No reply.

"So, you aren't going to tell me where you were?" he demands.

Marissa shakes her head and laughs in disbelief.

"Honestly, you are in no position to question me about anything," she replies.

Carson corners Marissa against the counter's edge. Yes, he messed up. Yes, he'd have to work really hard to get them back on track, but there was a line. He was not going to take her talking to him like this.

When he speaks he is face is inches from her face. His voice is slow and deliberate.

"Where were you, Mar?"

Marissa looks away defiantly. Carson grabs her shoulders and Marissa violently shrugs him off.

"Don't *even–*" she spits between clenched teeth.

She moves to get away from her husband, but Carson grabs her arm, admittedly harder than he should.

"Tell me where you were!" he demands.

Marissa manages to wrench her way free from his grasp. She slaps him, a little out of fear, mostly out of anger and throws him an acrimonious glare so heated a glimpse would instantly melt even the most resistant polar ice cap.

Still, Carson's ego won't let him back down.

"I deserve an explanation!" he shouts.

"No baby, that's my line!"

Her words sting more than her slap and physically cause him to step back as though he's been shoved. The frigid silence between them is colder than death as they stare each other down.

Silence.

She wants to hit him. He needs to hold her.   A boundary has been sundered; a threshold irrevocably crossed. The vows that they exchanged before family, friends and God seem so far removed in this moment.

Fear is the unspoken emotion that they share as time ticks on.

CHAPTER EIGHTEEN

"You were doing things with her that I taught you…"

Marissa stops talking and looks away as she feels herself beginning to tear up. She knows that now is not the time to cry; she has to remain strong.

"I can't do this now," she finally says. "I just came to get some things."

Conflicted, Carson glances at his watch. He really does need to get going as well, but he doesn't want them to leave things like this. He closes his eyes as if to send a silent prayer for strength. His tone is calmer when he speaks.

"This running away thing isn't going to fix this Mar?" he says. "We've got to talk…"

Rather than respond Marissa quickly walks out the kitchen and heads up the stairs. She knows that she can't be here; not while she is losing the fight against her tears. Sensing her husband watching her Marissa pauses part way up the staircase. She looks back at Carson, who stands doleful at the foot of the stairs.

His eyes are sad.

Her heart is broken.

A moment passes between them. Marissa swallows hard, turns her back on Carson and continues up the stairs.

CHAPTER NINETEEN

Carson is in his office at Sonic Studios in Hollywood. He is clearly distracted. The paperwork in front of him seems like a blur. He pushes back from his desk and turns in his executive chair to look out his corner office window. The 27th floor gives him an expansive view of the Miracle Mile strip below and the Hollywood sign in the distance.

Carson is so in his own world that he doesn't hear Jacob knock on the partially open door.

As always, Jacob is the image of GQ perfection in his custom Armani suit.

"Yo! Carson!"

Startled, Carson turns around to face his friend of a dozen plus years. His face shows no reprieve from his sadness.

"Hey," he sighs. "What's up, J?"

Carson gathers some paperwork and motions for Jacob to sit down.

"Are you all right?" Jacob asks. "How's Marissa?"

Carson sets aside his work and shakes his head.

"I don't want to say that it's over, but-"

"Didn't y'all talk?" Jacob asks.

"She hit me."

"What??? What happened?" Jacob asks in disbelief. "I thought you two were like this."

He gives the universal sign of being inseparable.

"Not anymore," Carson replies. "Not anymore."

Jacob looks at his friend in question. He's known Carson and Marissa forever and has been there through all of their ups and down. Jacob was having a hard time wrapping his head around this.

There's been a few times where he was sure they wouldn't make it, but they always pulled through as a couple. He was sure that nothing could tear them apart...except...

"What did you do?" Jacob asks. "Bro, what did you do?"

Carson gets up from his desk. He rubs his forehead in frustration as he paces the office.

"To say I'm a sphincter would be putting it nicely," Carson says. His voice is clearly stressed.

Jacob turns in his chair to watch his friend. He's still having trouble believing that his friend's relationship has come to this.

"Seriously, C," he asks, "What happened?"

"Truth," Carson replies, "It's no excuse, but lately Mar's always away on business. It was hi and bye when she was in town. I mean, Jake, we were supposed to be trying to have a baby, but instead we were becoming more like roommates than man and wife."

Jacob doesn't like where this if going. He stands up to face his friend.

"What did you do, Carson?"

Carson stops pacing. He closes his eyes momentarily in shame.

"I messed up," he replies. "Big time."

There's a knock at the door. Both men look over and see Franchesca standing in the doorway. She looks nervously from Carson to Jacob and then back to Carson.

"Hey," she says. "You got a moment?"

"It's not a good time," Carson replies.

"It's important."

Her eyes continue to dart back and forth between the two men. Jacob clears his throat.

"It's okay," Jacob says. "I'll come back. I gotta check on Kane anyways. Franchesca when you get a moment come by my office. If you're serious about this showcase we've got to talk."

"Sure," she replies.

"I'll holler at you later, J," Carson says.

"Do that."

Carson walks Jacob over to the door and closes it after he leaves. Now it's Franchesca's turn to pace the room.

"Well…"

"Well, what?" Carson says.

Franchesca stops pacing and turns to face Carson.

How could he be so nonchalant about this, she wonders.

"Did she come home?" she asks.

Carson goes back to his desk and sits down.

"Eventually," he replies. "But she's not talking to me. It's over."

"I'm sure it's not over, Carson," Franchesca challenges.

"I'm talking about you and me," Carson says matter-of-factly. "It never should have gotten this far."

"Whoa! Wait a minute," Franchesca protests. "You came after me remember."

"I was drunk."

"The first time…"

"You're her best friend," Carson points out.

"And you are her *husband*…Today anyways."

Carson shoots Franchesca a dirty look.

Without missing a beat Franchesca takes a seat across from Carson at his desk. Though ready with a quick retort if he was to say another word, her face softens as she sees the genuine sadness in his eyes.

She reaches across the desk and covers his hands with hers. Carson almost pulls away, but the human contact is soothing. He leaves his hand there and looks across at her.

"Look," Franchesca says. "You want to put us on ice? Fine, but I know Marissa and she is not going to just take you back, Carson. You're going to need someone in your corner."

"I could say the same for you," he replies.

Franchesca pulls her hand back and looks around nervously. She gets up and walks to the window.

"How much does Jacob know?"

"Only that Marissa and I fell out last night and that she didn't come home."

"Wait a minute I thought you said she did?"

"This morning," Carson replies. "Get this she won't tell me where she spent the night."

"She probably stayed at a hotel," she says quietly.

"I checked," Carson replies. "Nothing was charged to our cards. No ATM withdrawals. Nada."

He sits back in his chair in a frustrated sigh.

"Whenever we've had a fight she always goes to your house," he continues. "She cools out and then always comes home before bed. Never go to bed angry. It's a rule we have…had."

Franchesca turns from the window and says, "Well, we both know why that didn't hold up."

They hold each other's gaze a few moments longer than is probably appropriate. There is a breath of lust and loss, but they both quickly snap out of it.

"I love my wife, Frankie," Carson says.

"And I do too," Franchesca replies. "Both of you…but… I can't have you. Right now, I can't even work with you…not like this."

Carson stands up, unsure of where this is going.

Franchesca lets out a deep sigh and continues as she walks over to the office door preparing to leave.

"I'm just going deal with Jacob from now on. It'll be easier that way," she says quietly.

"I understand," he says quietly as he crosses the room.

He kisses her on the forehead. For an instant their lips are tempted to take it further. Carson steps back and Franchesca opens the door.

"I'm not asking you to make it easier on me," he says.

Franchesca turns back to face him.

"Foolish boy," she says endearingly, "Who said any of this was about you?"

CHAPTER TWENTY

The melancholy sounds of Sade's greatest hits fill the luxury en suite of the Winter's home. Her sad lyrics infused with the silken bubbles serve as a soothing comfort to a heartbroken Marissa.

Though the clock on the wall indicates it's probably too early for alcohol, a glass of white wine and half empty bottle of her favorite Pinot stand nearby as she bathes. Marissa soaks with her eyes closed. She needs this. From time to time, Sebastian crosses her mind. He really was a good friend to her in her time of need.

She smiles to herself, remembering the way he looked in the night air by her car wasn't so bad either.

The phone rings.

Marissa breaks from her daydream and instinctively reaches for her mobile phone. It's a number that she doesn't recognize.

"Hello?" she says, cautiously.

"So you made it home."

It's Sebastian, but he sounds angry.

Marissa sits up in the bath, surprised to hear his voice.

"Sebastian," she says. "How did you get this-"

"You don't remember? You gave me your card," he says. "I called your office and they said that you weren't in… I was worried about you."

Marissa takes a nervous sip of her wine.

"I'll be fine."

"You don't sound fine," Sebastian replies. His anger gives way to concern. "Are you okay? What happened?"

Marissa sighs. She's still a little bothered by how he initially came at her, but decides to set it aside for the moment. She uses a nearby towel to wrap herself as she gets out of the tub.

"He was waiting for me when I got in," she says as she towels off. "He had the nerve to *demand* to know where I had spent the night."

Sebastian is on the sofa in his luxury suite at the hotel, watching television as he listens.

"What did you tell him?" he asks.

"Nothing," Marissa replies.

88

Sebastian chuckles to himself.

"What?" Marissa says. "There's nothing to tell."

"Hmmm… I'm sure you could spin it to make him jealous," Sebastian says slyly.

Marissa is in her bedroom getting dressed. Her walk-in closet looks more like a designer boutique. She selects a Chanel tee to go with her Seven jeans. It's a mix and match moment, but she's feeling casual.

"Trust me," she says into the phone. "My husband isn't someone you want after you."

Silence.

"Sebastian?"

"I'm here."

Marissa's voice is quiet, almost vulnerable when she speaks.

"Thank you."

"For what?"

"Listening," she says.

"I'm a bartender.   It's what I do," he replies. "And I don't scare easy."

Sebastian turns the television off and goes to the patio door.   He looks outside at nothing in particular.   It's the sound of her voice that is of most interest to him.

"Hmm…" She sounds intrigued.

Sebastian paces himself, ensuring that his words fall in a natural rhythm.

"I'm curious," he says. "What are you going to do now?"

There is a moment of silence.   Sebastian waits patiently.   He's been here before.

Marissa sinks onto the edge of her bed. She catches her reflection in the mirror. The sadness in her eyes is almost too much. She brushes away a silent tear.

"I can't stay here," she replies quietly.

There is another moment of silence. Sebastian's timing is almost too perfect.

"Well, the room's here whenever you need it and so am I," Sebastian says. "Just call…"

He leans against the glass. His voice has an ominous tone.

"I'll always be there."

CHAPTER TWENTY-ONE

Jacob is in his office listening to the latest Kane demo. It's a hot urban track reminiscent of DMX at the height of his music career. He nods along with the beat.

The artist, Kane, is seated across from Jacob. While Kane could be considered good looking, if he lost the scowl, clearly he's a thug's thug who appears older than he really is. The grind of street life weighs as stress lines on his young face.

Right now, he shifts nervously watching Jacob; trying to read his face.

Jacob turns of the stereo mid-track.

"Okay," Jacob says. "I've heard it and you've got something. The question is what's it going to take for us to get you radio ready."

Kane is confused.

"You don't like it?"

"Didn't say that; it's just that music is changing," Jacob explains. "The music is hot. My producers will get you that all day. I'm more concerned with your lyrics."

"It's my life."

"That *was* your life," Jacob replies. "I'm sure you have dreams. Things you want to accomplish in life."

Kane pauses to think before answering.

"Yeah, of course there are," he says.

"So put it on wax," Jacob says. "This gun talk is great for the block, but radio won't touch it."

Kane looks at the ground.

"What is it?" Jacob asks.

"I'm not selling out, man."

"And we don't want you to," Jacob replies. "What we want is for you to be successful."

Jacob pauses for effect.

"You *do* want to be successful, don't you, Kane?"

Kane looks up at Jacob and adjusts his position in the chair.

"That's all I want," he replies.

"Good. Write some positive songs," Jacob says. "Songs about getting out of the hood and what life is like now. Write some songs for the ladies. Give me something to break radio with. We've got the streets covered. If you're gonna spend more of my money on making music I need hits that'll guarantee that I get it back."

He points at the stereo with the remote.

"This right here is a street anthem. Get these other songs together," he continues. "Me and Frankie are locking down the final details for your showcase. Do this right and you'll be a multi-millionaire before the year is through."

Kane finally smiles.

"I like the sound of that," Kane says, nodding.

"I thought you might," Jacob replies. "Now go write a song about it."

There's a knock at the office door.

"Come in!" Jacob shouts.

Carson enters as Kane gets up.

"Hey Kane," he says with a smile. "How's the record coming?"

Kane shrugs, but his voice is hopeful.

"Gotta write more songs," he replies.

"Ain't that always the way," Carson says. "Good luck to you."

Kane leaves and Carson closes the office door.

"For real," Carson says. "How is his record coming?"

Jacob shrugs indifferently.

"We'll see," he replies. "It's the same conversation every time. Franchesca says she's going to talk to him as well."

Carson stiffens at the mention of her name.

"What? You don't think that's a good idea?"

"No, no that's cool," Carson says. "She's his pet project, right?"

Jacob is a little suspicious of his friend's nervousness.

"Riiiight," Jacob says gingerly. "So you talked to Marissa, again?"

Carson sits down.

"Called a couple times but…"

Jacob waits for Carson to finish, but he never does.

"Alrighty then," Jacob says. "So, Franchesca says-"

"Huh?"

Jacob is really confused by Carson's jumpiness.

"I was saying, Franchesca said that since we're already in bed on the showcase she wants me to be stay on as the primary for Kane's project rather than handing it off to you for the polish."

Carson is still obviously distracted.

"Oh, yeah?" he says absently. "That's a good idea. I'm thinking about focusing on getting an R&B act together anyways."

"Really?" Jacob asks. "You hadn't mentioned that before."

"I know," Carson says. "I've been thinking about it for the last few nights. I figure if we can get a diversified roster together by summer we'll be good until Christmas."

"Anyone in mind?" Jacob asks.

"Nah," Carson replies. "I've got some demos. You know…might grab someone to open for Kane."

"Right."

Time to shift gears, Jacob thinks.

"So tell me what happened with you and Marissa?" Jacob asks. "I asked Frankie if she knew anything and she said to ask you. Now if your wife's best friend isn't talking then whatever you've done has got to be BAD!"

Carson is quiet. He looks at the back of his hands and braces himself for the backlash.

"I messed up big time, brother," he says quietly. "Broke my vows."

Jacob is beyond surprised by this revelation. Sure the industry is full of temptation, but Carson has always worshipped the ground Marissa walked on from the time they were college.

"Nah, man," Jacob says. "You're always here and I ain't seen a breezy that looks better than Marissa."

"Yeah, well... I did it... Mar found out... and she's pissed."

"And has every right to be!" Jacob adds, emphatically. "That's some mess that I would do, dude. Who'd you shag anyways?"

"That's not the point," Carson says. "What matters now is that I have to figure out how to save my marriage. You? You're a confirmed bachelor. This life was made for you... I can't see my life without, Marissa. There's just no point in it."

"That's what I'm tripping off of, C," Jacobs says. "You gotta tell me. With all the honeys that pass through these doors *who* on Earth could get you to stray?"

There's a knock at the door. Jacob signals to hold that thought.

"Come in!"

Franchesca opens the door, folder in hand, but stops short when she sees Carson.

"Sorry," she says. "Bad timing. I'll come back."

Jacob stands up.

"No, no, uh, Carson," he says. "We can talk later. Frankie and I were going to-"

"Get a bite to eat," Franchesca quickly says, adding, "And go over the Kane project. I've got that list of sub-promoters."

Carson looks back and forth between the two of them. Something is off, but he can't put his finger on it.

"All right," he says. "Just stay within budget. I'll get out of here. Maybe I'll even go home early."

"That sounds good," Jacob says.

"Great idea," Franchesca adds.

She and Jacob look at one another and then back at Carson.

"Hey, get out of here," Jacob says. "Fix things with your wife. Tell her me and Frankie say what's up."

Franchesca swallows hard and looks away. There's no missing that. Jacob cocks his head to the side and looks at the both of them.

"What?" he asks.

"I gotta go," Carson says.

He slips out of the office before Jacob can stop him. On his way to his office, Carson pulls out his mobile phone and dials his home number.

CHAPTER TWENTY-TWO

Marissa is asleep on the chaise lounge in the guestroom. An empty bottle of wine and a wedding album are on the floor next to her. Carson has been standing over her for at least fifteen minutes.

He gently nudges his wife to wake her.

"Marissa," he says softly. "Mar… Marissa, honey, wake up."

Marissa slowly stirs and looks up to see her husband.

"You fell asleep."

Looking around her eyes glance over the empty wine bottle but stop on the wedding album. Her combination of rage and gloom quickly returns. Marissa brushes past Carson without a word.

"Marissa!" Carson calls after her. "Come on, we've to talk about this. Babe, please."

He follows after her through the house. She's in the living room pacing.

"Mar," he says.

"One look at you and I can't even breathe."

"I'm sorry."

"Shut up."

"Marissa."

"Shut up! You don't get to be in control," she spits at him. "Not now. Not about this."

Carson's shoulders droop as he begins to accept that his will not be an easy fix or a matter of simple forgiveness. He sinks into the couch waiting for Marissa to speak.

The clock ticks on and no one speaks. Carson tries on several occasions to say something, but Marissa shakes her head to discourage a conversation every time.

Finally, she stops moving long enough to ask the one question that has been on her mind from the moment she first caught him...them.

"Why my best friend?"

"Huh?"

His lack of an intelligible answer only serves to anger her more.

"Why...my...best...friend?" she repeats.

Her look is cold and tone is full of impatience.

"I mean, you must have really wanted to hurt me," she continues.

"It wasn't like that, Mar," Carson says.

"Really??? I walked in on you and Frankie IN OUR BED! IN OUR BED, CARSON!" she shouts. "What the hell! I mean, you were doing things with her that I taught you! How long has this been going on?"

"I'm sorry," Carson said sullenly.

"I asked you a question."

"I know," he replies. "I'm sorry."

"You said that already."

"Because I am," Carson says.

He searches her face for any sign of forgiveness.

"Not good enough."

None exists.

Marissa crosses her arms and walks to the front bay window.

"What do you want me to do?" Carson asks. "How do we fix this… fix us? I swear, Mar, counseling, whatever you want."

Marissa keeps her back to him. More silence. Carson gets fed up and decides to change the course of this conversation. He reaches into his pocket and produces a Tiffany ring box.

"I bought you something," he says quietly.

Marissa opens the ring box to reveal a pink diamond ring that would make even J.Lo jealous.

"How Kobe of you," Marissa says dryly. "However, you should never apologize to your wife with expensive jewelry."

"What do you mean? Why not?"

Marissa forcefully hands the gift box back.

"It'll only make her wonder what you bought your mistress."

Carson is stunned.

"I need a drink," Marissa says.

"A drink," Carson replies. "That's a good idea."

He goes into the kitchen to retrieve a couple of glasses and a bottle of Grey Goose. When Carson returns he stops short, stunned.

Marissa is gone.

CHAPTER TWENTY-THREE

The Version Lounge is crowded tonight. The band is in full swing covering Maxwell's "Cococure". Sebastian is at the bar serving u drinks to the locals. Marissa enters and makes her way to the bar. She manages to grab a stool, just as a patron vacates it, next to the bar.

Sebastian sees her sit down. He smiles at her. Marissa gives him a small wave.

He quickly finishes serving a few other customers before coming over to Marissa with a drink. Grey Goose and Seven.

"You remembered," she says with a smile.

"That's my job," he replies. "How are you feeling?"

"I hate him," Marissa says and takes a sip of her beverage. "I hate both of them."

Sebastian senses an opportunity.

"Need to crash again?"

Marissa takes another sip, longer this time, as she considers the offer and then looks up at Sebastian.

"I'd like that," she replies and then smiles. "Can you fix all of my problems?"

"You got it."

Sebastian starts to walk away.

110

"Hey, Sebastian?" Marissa calls after him.

Sebastian comes back over. She swallows hard as she gathers some courage before speaking.

"Later on…dance with me?"

"You have no idea of what I'm willing to do for you."

CHAPTER TWENTY-FOUR

It's nearly closing time. The band is playing a George Benson number. The lights are low and the room almost empty. Sebastian holds Marissa close as they dance slowly; her head upon his shoulder. His hand delicately rests at the small of his back

She is sad in her heart, but this moment brings her peace. Sebastian can feel her need and holds her closer. He gently kisses the top of her head as they continue to dance.

CHAPTER TWENTY-FIVE

Sebastian and Marissa enter his hotel suite laughing. It's late. Very late. Marissa hasn't laughed like this in a long time. Sebastian takes her jacket from her and points the direction to the main room.

He takes her overnight bag and sets it inside his bedroom.

"You want some tea?" he asks. "I don't drink coffee."

Marissa crashes on the couch. The alcohol has relaxed her mood. She's not drunk, however she is feeling very good right now.

"Tea would be nice," she says.

Sebastian soon returns with a cup for each of them. Time has passed and Marissa is a little sleepy. Sebastian smiles at her, comfortably curled up on the couch as he sets the cups on the table.

"You're cute when you're drunk," he says.

"Shows what you know, Mr. Bartender," Marissa replies. "I'm not drunk. I'm happy. Tired, but happy… You make me happy."

Sebastian smiles as he sits next her. One arm over the back of the couch he faces Marissa.

"If only we could do something about you being married," he says.

Marissa shakes her head in denial.

"I don't want to talk about that."

"Just saying."

"And I'm saying-"

Sebastian puts his hands up in self-defense.

"Okay, okay," he says in mock protest. "Drink you tea. I'll put a movie on."

Sebastian kisses her forehead. Marissa takes her tea and smiles.

"Good idea," she says.

Sebastian turns on the television.

"Look at that," he says. "A Bond marathon. I love Bond."

"Very sexy," Marissa replies.

Sebastian laughs.

"Drink up, Lush."

CHAPTER TWENTY-SIX

Sebastian and Marissa have fallen asleep. The television is still on and a random paid programming segment is on. Sebastian and Marissa have managed to end up cuddled together on the sofa. Sebastian has his arms around Marissa and pulls her closer in his sleep.

A change in volume from the program to a commercial causes both of them to stir. Sleepily, Marissa looks up at Sebastian. He half-smiles through partially closed eyes.

"Hey," she says sleepily.

"Hey."

Sebastian kisses Marissa's forehead as they adjust on the couch. Their movement brings them closer together. Though cautiously at first, Sebastian leans in and softly kisses Marissa. She doesn't pull away as they exchange a series of brief kisses. Sooner than later their kisses become more intense.

Marissa pauses.

"We should stop," she says.

Even as she speaks she knows that that is not going to happen. They continue kissing. This time Sebastian pulls back.

"We should," he says. "You're married."

They continue kissing. Each kiss becomes more passionate in the resemblance of appreciative lovers rather than newfound friends.

"Someone should have-" she says breathlessly.

Another kiss.

"told my…"

Another kiss.

"husband that, when…"

Another kiss.

"he slept with my best friend."

Sebastian pulls away from Marissa for a moment. He searches her face for any sign of objection. There is a sadness in her eyes, but more than that a need.

"I'll do anything you want tonight," he says softly. "No strings."

Marissa manages a bare whisper when she answers, "I just want to forget, even if it's just for one night… Just help me forget."

Moments later, Sebastian and Marissa are in the master bedroom. The window is ajar allowing for a gentle night breeze to flutter the sheer curtains in the moonlight. The energy is one of a conflicted romance. Lust, sadness, desire and pain amalgamate in an esoteric fashion as they fall intertwined to the oversized custom framed bed.

Sebastian pulls Marissa up to a seated position and pauses to look in her eyes. There passion is caution in the first few moments. Sebastian removes his shirt between kisses.

While it appears that Sebastian is the master in this engage, Marissa's eyes profess a far different tale. She raises her hands above her head allowing him to easily remove her Chanel tee.

The sadness is fading. This excites Sebastian. Kissing more passionately now, they fall back onto the oversized pillows.

Marissa giggles.

Sebastian smiles.

"You okay?" he asks, breathing heavily.

"Yeah," she answers, equally breathless. "I'm with you."

CHAPTER TWENTY- SEVEN

The sun creeps through the open window of Sebastian's suite, casting a softened glow on the resting couple. Sebastian watches Marissa as she sleeps, stroking her arm. After a while Marissa stirs.

"Hey," he smiles.

"Hey yourself," Marissa replies. "Damn, how many times was that?"

Sebastian reaches for a pack of cigarettes from the bedside locker. He casually removes one and places it between his lips.

"Lost count somewhere after the third and forth go 'round," he chuckles. "Or was it the fifth and sixth?"

Sebastian offers Marissa a cigarette. She smiles, but shakes his head.

"I don't smoke."

Sebastian lights up and takes a deep drag. He slowly expels the smoke and grows serious.

"What's wrong?" Marissa asks.

Sebastian hesitates. He doesn't want to lose this moment, but they do need to talk.

"Oh," she says it suddenly hits her. She knows where this is going.

"I'm trying to decide what we should do about the pink elephant in the room?" he says.

"I told you…I mean," Marissa says. "You said… no strings…"

"I know."

He takes another drag and expels the smoke before continuing.

"Still, Mar," he says. "You've got to admit that we have… a connection."

"That's true," she replies. There is no point in denying the obvious. "You're probably the best friend that I have right now."

Sebastian smiles.

"I think you're pretty cool too," he says.

"But…"

Sebastian looks at her left hand.

"But, you're married."

Marissa looks down and sees her wedding ring staring back accusingly at her. She looks at Sebastian and then back to her ring. It is time to make a decision. Marissa removes her wedding ring and places it on the nightstand.

"Not today," she says.

"That easy, huh?"

"That's a question for-"

Sebastian motions for her to be quiet. He voice is firm, with a frightening chill.

"Shhh," he says. "Never speak his name around here. Ever. You're with me now."

Marissa is taken aback by Sebastian's authoritative tone, but at the same time she finds his firmness to be a cool aphrodisiac.

Sebastian takes another deep drag of his cigarette and then forcefully puts it out. It is like watching her own personal James Dean in action.

"I'm glad you have decided to stay," he says. "I'd hate to have to chase you."

Sebastian is gentle, yet adamantine in his next amative overture. Marissa slowly parts her lips and genially accepts his invitation.

CHAPTER TWENTY-EIGHT

Carson is swimming the length of his pool. Though his form shows a coached technique there is an obvious frustration in each stroke. As he comes back from his fourth trip to the deep-end Carson sees a pair of brand new Alexander McQueen's standing at the edge of the pool. When he reaches the lip of the pool, Carson stops swimming and looks up.

It's Jacob.

"You're early," Carson says, wiping the water from his eyes.

"Your wife is missing," Jacob replies. "I put the word out. Nothing back yet, though."

Carson nods and Jacob steps back so that Carson can lift himself out of the pool. He gestures for Jacob to hand him a towel. Jacob tosses him a towel from the nearby table and Carson begins to towel off.

"So what are we thinking?" Jacob asks.

Still toweling off, Carson walks into the house and Jacob casually follows behind him. They make their way through the kitchen into the adjacent home gym.

"Truth is, I can't even say," Carson replies. "She's due back at work today, but I can't ambush her."

"Why not?" Jacob asks in disbelief.

"Come on, Bro-"

"Fine," Jacob says. "That doesn't mean that I can't stop in or better yet Franchesca."

Carson stiffens slightly at the mention of his ex-lover's name.

"What's that about?" Jacob asks. "You okay?"

Still distracted, Carson steps into the adjoining dressing room.

"I'll be better when my wife comes home," he grunts.

Carson emerges from the dressing room in shorts and a tee. He jumps on the treadmill.

"Let's put in an hour," he says. "Then we'll go and look for her."

CHAPTER TWENTY-NINE

Clearly it is going to be no more than a half day for Marissa. Walking out of the hotel towards her Mercedes, Marissa pauses when her mobile phone rings indicating an incoming text message.

She flips open the phone to reveal the message. She smiles to herself and begins to text back.

"I miss you already, too," she says to herself as she writes.

She presses send and puts the phone back into her purse. Had she looked back she would have seen Sebastian standing on the balcony watching her.

There was mildly disturbing glint in his eye.

CHAPTER THIRTY

Marissa is hard at work. She has unfinished Chinese take-out on her desk amidst some random paperwork. The outer office area is buzzing with excitement. She doesn't need the noise.

She gets up from her desk to close her office door. It's not quite closed when there is a knock at the door.

"Oh," she says stepping back.

She opens the door. It's Jacob.

"Can I come in?" he asks.

"You may," she says returning to her desk in a confident stride. "I'm not going to insult you by asking why you're here. However, I must tell you that I don't really want to hear it, Jacob."

Jacob clears his throat.

"I can respect that," he replies. "I may not know all the facts but at least let me plead my man's case before you throw me out."

"The facts are simple, J," Marissa says not missing a beat. "I'm clear, he's clear and I really don't need to go over them again."

Jacob throws up his hands feigning mock defeat.

"All right. Okay."

Jacob gestures in question towards a chair opposite of Marissa's desk. She responds with a hand gesture that indicates that she's not going to stop him if he does.

He sits.

"Thanks," he says. "So is it cool if you and I just talk? It's been a minute since we've done that... I remember a time when we were pretty close you and me."

"Yeah, well... Being a grown-up means we don't get to play as much we'd like," Marissa replies. "Some of us anyways."

"Ouch. Is that directed at me or your man?"

Marissa doesn't reply, instead she pretends to be focusing on her work.

"Two birds, one stone I suppose," Jacob says.

Marissa chuckles to herself.

"Something like that," she says.

"That's what I love about your, Mar," Jacob says.

Marissa looks up at him.

"What's that?"

"You don't waste any time."

"I could say the same for your mate," she retorts.

"Touché."

Marissa sets her work aside and focuses on Jacob. He smiles that friendly smile that lets her know that his is her friend as well, and always will be.

"Okay," he says. "Seriously now… How are you?"

Marissa sits back, sighs in a laborious tone and looks out of the window for a moment before returning her gaze to Jacob. There is a knock at the door again. This time it is

Marissa's chipper assistant, Cynthia. She enters with a fabulous bouquet of flowers.

"Hey boss," she says. "These just came for you. They look amazing!"

Cynthia hands Marissa the card and places the flowers on the table.

"Thank you, Cynthia," Marissa says.

Cynthia exits the office and Marissa opens the card.

It says: "We're really good together. Dinner? Love, S"

Marissa smiles.

CHAPTER THIRTY-ONE

Carson is leaning against Jacob's Jag, on his mobile phone. He appears to be in a deep conversation. Jacob comes out of the distinguished office tower and heads over to his car. Seeing Jacob, Carson quickly ends his call.

"I gotta go," he says and hangs up.

Carson puts away his phone and looks at Jacob expectantly.

"So what happened?" he asks. "What did she say? She wanna talk? Should I go in there? What's up?"

Jacob waves his friend off.

"Slow down," Jacob says. "Get in the car. You, my friend, have *a lot* of work to do."

Jacob gets into the driver side of his Jaguar and Carson hops into the passenger side. Jacob checks his gauges as he starts the car.

"Okay, just answer me this," Carson says. "On the record – does she hate me?"

"On the record... right now that'd be a yes," Jacob replies.

Carson winces.

"Okay, what about off?"

"Off the record?" Jacob says pulling out of the lot. "She doesn't really hate you. She's hurt."

138

Carson ponders this for a moment.

"So I should talk to her?"

"I said she doesn't hate you," Jacob replies. "I didn't say that she wanted to see you."

Carson is quiet as they drive for a while. For this time of day, traffic is surprisingly modest. They head towards Sunset Blvd. After some time a far more demure Carson speaks.

"Did she tell you what happened?" he asks.

"Nah," Jacob replies. "She didn't want to talk about it and honestly, I wasn't going to pry."

"But you were in there forever… What did y'all talk about?"

"Do you trust me?" Jacob asks.

"What?"

"I said do you trust me?"

"Of course I trust you. You're my best fri...Where are you going with this?"

"Okay. You trust me," Jacob says. "Now, do you trust that I'm a guy who knows a lot about women?"

"C'mon, J."

"I asked you a question," Jacob says as he turns into their company's private lot.

"Jake, you're like the only playboy that makes King Heph jealous," Carson answers. "Yes, you know women!"

"Well, first thing. Good look on sending the flowers," Jacob says. "She was definitely impressed."

Carson is confused.

"What flowers?" he asks. "I didn't send any flowers."

"You didn't?"

"No."

Jacob sighs as he pulls into his assigned space.

"Well, that being said there is one thing I know above all when it comes to women and today this truism couldn't have been more on point," he says. "Especially, if you didn't buy those flowers."

"Oh, yeah," Carson says. "What's that?"

"Today, I did the one thing every woman needs."

Carson grows alarmed.

"Don't tell me you did my wife, J?!?!"

Jacob chuckles to himself.

"Okay, the other thing," he says.

"What?"

Jacob gives Carson that, *"See this is why you are in the situation you're in right now"* look.

Carson stares expectantly for his friend to enlighten him.   Jacob shakes his head disbelief.

"I listened, man," Jacob replies, "and believe me when I say you better start listening too 'cause me, I'm your boy. You ain't never got to worry about me trying to bag your girl."

Carson grows even more concerned.

"What are you trying to say?" he asks.

A sobering moment passes between friends as they walk towards the office.

"Truth?" Jacob asks.

"Always."

Jacob takes a deep breath.

"All right," he says. "Fact is we don't know where Marissa has been these last couple days, but I got the feeling that wherever she was someone was listening to her. It was a bad ass bouquet, bro."

Jacob lets a weighted moment pass before continuing.

"Don't let that conversation get too deep."

CHAPTER THIRTY-TWO

The main lights in Marissa's office are off. Only a modest desktop lamp and the illumination provided by the flat screen television provided her any light.

Reclining on the office sofa Marissa is taking a moment to relax on the phone after an aggressive workday.

She's talking with Sebastian.

"I want to," Marissa says. "I'd love to, but I can't."

"Come on," Sebastian pleads. "Have a quick drink. See what happens."

"That sounds nice," she replies in a reflective tone.

"You're nice."

"And married."

"I could help you forget about that," his voice is sly, "again… and again…and again…"

Flashbacks of their sexual exchange flash in her mind bringing a guilty smile to her lips. Just as quickly, her wedding band brings Marissa crashing back to reality.

"I've gotten my revenge, Sebastian," she says. "I have to go home sometime…"

She continues to finger her wedding band as they talk.

"Don't let him get off so easy, M," Sebastian says. His voice grows temptingly darker. "Punish him. Let me *help you* punish him."

Marissa considers it.

"I wish," she finally says. "I wish I could make them feel what I felt."

"I've got a couple ideas."

Marissa giggles. Sebastian remains quiet.

"Sebastian, you have been amazing, but…"

"Don't say it," Sebastian interjects. "It's bad enough that I'm the odd man out… The last thing I need is the P.C. kiss-off as well."

Now it's Marissa's turn to be quiet.

"Marissa?"

"I should go," she says. "I'm having words with her tonight."

"I could take care of everything for you. I could get rid of all your problems," Sebastian says. "You know it's what you want."

"I have to go."

Unbeknownst to Marissa, Sebastian is seated in his Escalade on his mobile phone, in her work's parking lot. A picture that he took of Marissa while she was sleeping is on the seat next to him. It was taken at an eerie angle that at first glance makes her look as though she might be dead.

"You are so beautiful," he says.

"Thanks," Marissa replies softly. "Hey, Sebastian?"

"Yeah?" he replies.

He sits up hopeful. There is a pause on the other end of the line. The sound of her breathing quickens his heart.

She sighs.

"Goodbye."

"No, Marissa," Sebastian replies. "I could never say goodbye to you, only good night."

He hangs up his phone before Marissa can speak. His demeanor changes as a subtle rage passes over his eyes. In the next moment it's gone, but definitely not forgotten.

Sebastian starts up his truck and then changes his mind. He turns off the engine and waits.

CHAPTER THIRTY-THREE

Franchesca is seated at a table in the back of Gardenia Restaurant, favorite celebrity hideaway. Several of Hollywood's who's who are dining here tonight.

Marissa enters the restaurant. She is looking around, taking everything in when her eyes stop on Franchesca. At first there is a level of distaste in her gaze, but Marissa quickly changes it to one of renewed resolve.

She takes a deep breath and walks over.

"You made it," she says.

Franchesca is startled, but manages a "please forgive me" smile.

"Hey.   Yeah, this," she stammers. "Fixing this... It's important to me."

"Mmm hmm," Marissa says.

She pulls out her chair and sits opposite of Franchesca.

"I won't ask how you've been," Franchesca says.

"That would be wise."

There is a long silence as the ladies look over the menus before them. Marissa motions for the waiter to come over. He looks like newbie actor, paying his dues.

"Good evening, ladies," the waiter says. "What can I get for you?"

"I'll have a white wine," Marissa replies. "She'll have a Starfucker."

The waiter nods matter-of-factly and walks away.

"I deserve that," Franchesca says.

"I'd say you deserve more than that," Marissa retorts in a harsh whisper. "After all, I only caught you in bed with *my husband*."

Silence.

"No response," Marissa sneers. "Of course not. The whole thing... it's just whatever to you, right?"

Franchesca fusses with her napkin on the table. She struggles to look Marissa in her eyes.

"I know you Marissa," she says. "Me apologizing isn't going to make it any better. So, yeah... in a way it is whatever with me...

with you. Whatever you need to make this right, I'm here... I'm here and I'm sorry."

Franchesca feels herself beginning to well up but continues.

"I don't expect you to make it easy for me," she says. "In fact, if I were you I wouldn't even be talking to me. I just -"

"Shut up, okay," Marissa interjects completely annoyed by Franchesca's rambling. "Just shut up. Just quit. Quit with the all of the bloody I statements before I give you one. I, I, I... News flash – This isn't about you!"

"I'm sorry."

"Fuck you."

More silence. Marissa glares at Franchesca. The waiter returns with their drinks, but sensing the obvious tension he tentatively places them on the table.

"Thank you," Marissa says confidently.

"Yes," Franchesca says quietly. "Thank you."

"Would you like to order dinner or will you just be having drinks," he asks nervously.

Franchesca looks to Marissa to make the decision.

"Just drinks, thanks."

"Okay. Enjoy."

The waiter scurries away to safety. There is more silence and the ladies hold each other's gaze.

"Don't hold your breath for a toast," Marissa finally says.

She slowly sips her wine knowing that each moment of silence is making Franchesca increasingly uncomfortable. Marissa watches her… waiting…

Franchesca hesitates before sipping her drink.

Still no words…

Marissa clears her throat.

CHAPTER THIRTY-FOUR

Outside the restaurant in the shadows Sebastian is standing… waiting… watching… There is a haunting, obsessive rage in his eyes.

It's now or never.

CHAPTER THIRTY-FIVE

Marissa and Franchesca are a few drinks into their meeting. There is still a heavy mood between them. Finally, Marissa takes a final swig and speaks.

"I should hate you," she says. "I did hate you, but I can't… not anymore. Can't steal second with your foot on first."

Franchesca is confused.

"Hating you doesn't help me," Marissa explains and clears her throat. "So here it is."

156

Franchesca shifts in her seat nervously.

"You and me? We are not friends. We're not enemies. WE are not *anything* and will not be anything unless I choose to change my mind," Marissa says. "See, it is about me now… and not just what I want, but what I need. What I want is for you to *stay away* from *my husband*, but your jobs preclude my wishes soooo… I need you to know that I will ensure that very, very bad things will happen to you if you even have involuntary personal *thoughts* towards *my husband*! Understand me when I say, my marriage is NOT… A… GAME!"

Marissa takes another quick yet confident swig, finishing her wine.

"Not another word," she says shortly. "I'll see you at the showcase."

She stands up.

"Be sure to tip nice."

Marissa turns and walks out the restaurant before a stunned Franchesca can respond.

Moments later the waiter arrives at the table with the bill.

CHAPTER THIRTY-SIX

Marissa exits the restaurant and waits for the valet to return with her car. Unbeknownst to her she is being watched. There is a feeling of nervousness as she checks her watch. Something is off.

When her car pulls up Marissa walks over to the driver side. She is taken aback when she sees who is driving…

It's Sebastian. He opens the door.

"Hi'ya doll," he says sweetly. "How was dinner?"

"What on Earth are you doing in my car?" Marissa asks alarmed. "Get out!"

Sebastian plays it cool, exits the car, but blocks Marissa from entering.

"You should have told me," he says. "We could have had dinner together. You know I wanted to see you. I've missed ya, babe."

He leans in to kiss her, but Marissa ducks his pass.

"Stop it," she says angrily. "What if I had been here with my husband?"

She attempts to push Sebastian aside. He laughs, but moves aside for her. Marissa angrily gets into her car and reaches for the door to close it, but Sebastian grabs it before it closes and leans into the car.

"I was there for you when you needed me," he seethes. "I've been the perfect man for you. I *am* the perfect man for you. You cannot... seriously...just... walk... away."

"It was one night, Sebastian," Marissa says. "I'm sorry. It was a mistake."

"It was *not* just one night and it was *not* a mistake and you know it," he retorts. "You begged me for it and I gave it to you good... You begged me to make you forget and I DID! You belong to me."

Sebastian steps back, but doesn't release the door from his grasp.

"It's real simple," he continues. "You chose me, Marissa. Don't make me chase you."

Sebastian blows a cynical kiss in her direction and lets go of the door. Marissa shuts the door and peels out of the parking lot as quickly as possible. Had she looked around she would have seen Franchesca exiting the restaurant. She looked after Marissa's retreating car and then back to the valet where Sebastian was confidently watching.

He looks over at Franchesca and smiles. He senses an opportunity.

CHAPTER THIRTY-SEVEN

Marissa pulls into the driveway of her home. It's late. Through the window she can see Carson in the living room. He's watching the television or rather the television is watching him.

Marissa watches through the window for a few moments as her husband sleeps. Though she is nervous, in her heart she knows that coming home is the right decision. Quietly, she goes inside.

Upon entering the living room, Marissa removes her jacket and places her briefcase on the floor. She sits quietly on the smaller chesterfield perpendicular to her sleeping husband and watches him.

It is only after some time has passed that Marissa realizes what is playing on the television. Carson had been watching the DVD of their wedding. Marissa moves to sit on the same chesterfield as her husband. It is then that she sees that in his arms he is cradling their wedding photo. Marissa is subtly moved.

"How did we get here?" she asks herself quietly.

Carson stirs. Seeing his wife next to him, he smiles.

"Hey," she says softly.

"Hey," Carson replies sleepily.

He sits ups, but remains cautious in his movements, not wanting to ruin this moment.

The couple holds each other's gaze for a long time. Tears begin to well in both of their eyes. A moment later they embrace in a desperate hug, weeping openly. No words are spoken as their tears attempt to wash away their pain.

The tears have stopped and the television has been turned off as to not offer any form of distraction. Marissa and Carson are seated facing each other on the chesterfield. There are two wine goblets and a half empty bottle of wine on the coffee table.

"I have questions, Carson," Marissa says. "*A lot* of questions."

Though he wants to speak up Carson heeds Jacob's advice and remains quiet. There is strength in Marissa's tone as she steels herself during this conversation.

"If we're going to get through this you'll have to answer them…"

"Okay," Carson replies.

"Completely… Honestly," she pauses. "Explicitly…"

Carson nods his understanding. Marissa reaches into his purse to produce an envelope.

"I've made a list," she says quietly.

The sound of a cab beeping the horn is heard. Marissa gets up from the chesterfield. Carson is confused.

"I'm not staying here tonight," Marissa explains.

She slowly hands her husband the envelope.

"I expect both of you to answer them," she says matter-of-factly.

Carson wants to say something, but his wife's exacted yet subtle confidence as she strides away shocks him into silence.

Marissa leaves Carson alone in the living room and leaves their home for the night. While she may appear to be the picture of confidence to her husband, what Carson doesn't see are the silent tears that stain her face as she walks out the door.

Alone with the envelope in his hands, Carson decides to review its contents.

CHAPTER THIRTY-EIGHT

Franchesca feels like she's been waiting forever since turning her ticket in to the valet. After the meeting with Marissa all she wants to do is go home and go to bed.

"This is ridiculous," she says to herself.

The attendants are usually quite prompt with bringing up the cars. Franchesca checks her watch again and contemplates going inside the restaurant to find a manager.

Suddenly from the back of the parking lot a different valet attendant comes running in a complete panic.

"What!" Franchesca asks. "Where the hell's my car?"

Moments later the restaurant is lit up like a Christmas tree courtesy of the patrol cars now on site. Franchesca, the valet attendants and police are standing at what was once Franchesca's impeccable Jaguar.

All of the windows, headlights and taillights have been smashed out. The car has been keyed within an inch of its life and kicked in beyond recognition.

"Ma'am?" the police officer says. "Ma'am?"

Franchesca is transfixed on the glaring act of revenge spray-painted across the side of her prized possession: WHORE!!!

"Ma'am?"

"Huh?" she answers, clearly in shock. "What?"

"Ma'am, I was asking you if you have any idea as to who might want to do this to you?" the officer asks.

Franchesca shakes her head.

"I... I... I don't... no, no officer," she stammers. "I don't know. I have no idea."

"Well," the officer says. "There have been some random acts of vandalism in the area, but this... This seems pretty personal."

"Well, I don't know what to tell you," she replies. "Never in a million years did I imagine ever coming out to this."

CHAPTER THIRTY-NINE

Marissa is exiting the Mondrian on Sunset early this morning. She feels good about her decisions and while she's not certain what the future holds she knows that for now she's going to be okay.

Marissa heads over to her car, a cup of coffee in hand. Being up, barely after the sun, make this cup of java her nearest and dearest friend. She wants to get into the office early to catch up on the work she had neglected the day before.

Things seem to be looking up for her. Marissa is about to get into her car when Sebastian suddenly appears from out of nowhere, holding a single rose. Marissa is rightfully startled.

"I'm sorry," he says with a smile.

"What the hell! Are you crazy? What are you doing here?"

"You didn't go back to him."

"Sebastian," Marissa says. "How did you know I was here?"

"Hey, forget it," he replies. "I just, I just wanted to apologize. I was out of my head last night. You're an amazing woman. I just wanted to see you once more. I didn't mean to trip out. You got to me, but I worked it out. You're a beautiful woman, Marissa, but you're married. I was wrong and I'm sorry."

Sebastian extends the rose in an olive branch fashion.

"Seriously," he continues. "I didn't mean to scare you."

Marissa tentatively accepts the flower.

"Thank you," she says quietly.

"You're still my favorite girl," Sebastian says. "I gotta run. Come by the lounge tonight. Friends… I've got a surprise for you; around nine. I'll see you later. Don't forget!"

Sebastian takes off before Marissa can respond.

CHAPTER FORTY

Carson stares at the stack of questions Marissa gave him sitting on his desk. Each question is so precise and explicit. The fact that she really wants both he and Franchesca to answer them only causes the nauseating pit in his stomach to grow exponentially.

The fact that it's nearly two o'clock in the afternoon and Franchesca *still* hasn't come into the office nor is she picking up her phone isn't helping either. Carson picks up his office phone receiver and tries her number again.

He listens impatiently as Franchesca's phone once again goes directly to voicemail.

"Franchesca. Carson," he says shortly. "We've got to talk. You've got to come by the office and help me fix this. I don't know where the hell you are today, but… Look, Mar and I talked and… Just… Just call me back."

Carson hangs up the phone and stares at the pages that seem to stare accusingly back at him.

"This is not good," he says to himself.

CHAPTER FORTY-ONE

Franchesca is standing at her bureau, putting on her day jewelry as she prepares to go out for what remains of the work day. She glances back at the man sleeping in her bed.

"Come on sleepyhead," she says with a smile. "You can't stay in bed all day."

Her gentleman caller pushes the covers back just enough to reveal his face. It's Jacob.

"I can if I want," he says. "You're the only appointment I have today."

Franchesca giggles quietly.

"Come back to bed," Jacob says seductively.

"I can't," she replies. "Your business partner slash my boss has been blowing up my mobile all morning."

"He probably wants you to talk to Marissa for him."

Franchesca stiffens and Jacob notices. He props himself up in the bed.

"Okay, what?" he asks.

"Nothing."

"I call Bullshavyck," Jacob says. "Come on, Frankie. What's going on?"

Franchesca takes a deep breath before speaking.

"It's nothing," she says. "I just can't believe someone *stole* my car…from bloody VALET! I mean, who does that???"

"Yeah," Jacob says. "I still don't get why you didn't just call me to come and pick you up. What were you doing at Gardenia's so late anyways? You cheatin' on me?"

Jacob chuckles to himself, but Franchesca quickly comes to the bedside. Jacob makes room for her to sit down. In an effort of distraction Franchesca changes the subject.

"Of course not, babe," she answers. "But, you know Carson's gonna flip when he finds out about us. Could make things complicated…"

Jacob playfully slips his hand up Franchesca's skirt.

"So, he doesn't find out," Jacob teases. "It's nobody's business but ours anyways."

"Stop it," she giggles. "Secrets are bad."

"What?" Jacob says in mock protest. "It's been almost a year, babe. We're not hurting anybody... Hmm?"

Franchesca finds it hard to focus as Jacob continues to slide his hand further up her inner thigh.

"Tell me," he says alluringly. "Does this hurt?"

Franchesca closes her eyes approaching ecstasy.

"No," she says breathlessly. "That feels pretty good actually."

Jacob leans over and kisses Franchesca. He begins massaging her inner thigh, his hand working its way higher and higher. Franchesca emits a soft yet seductive moan.

"I can make you feel really good," Jacob says temptingly. "All you've gotta do is come back to bed."

Before Franchesca can reply Jacob scoops her up and takes a position of advantage over her on the bed. Franchesca giggles with mischievous glee. He teases her with a few kisses.

"I've gotta go!" she laughs.

Jacob shakes his head.

"Come here," he growls.

They begin to kiss passionately. The phone by the bed rings. The call display indicates that it is the studio.

Neither lover notices.

CHAPTER FORTY-TWO

Simply put Carson is pissed. He can't find Jacob or Franchesca. No one has shown up to work and no one is answering their phones.

"Dammit!" he shouts. "Where is everybody today!?!?"

CHAPTER FORTY-THREE

Jacob and Franchesca are in the final throws of passion. All thoughts of work or stress were a million miles away. Franchesca rolls off of Jacob and sighs.

"Wow," Franchesca says exasperated.

"You can say that again," Jacob says, equally spent.

Franchesca checks the time. It's nearly three o'clock.

"You better call him," she says. "Tell him we're at lunch going over the budget."

"Sure," Jacob teases. "I must admit I do love running your numbers, girl."

Franchesca playfully tosses a pillow at Jacob. They kiss briefly and then she gets out of the bed to shower.

Jacob reaches for the phone and begins dialing.

CHAPTER FOURTY-FOUR

Carson and Kane are in the mixing room listening to the playback of the latest record. It's loud... Just the way that they like it.

"It's hot, right!" Kane shouts over the music.

"Yeah, this is it," Carson replied. "This is what we need for radio. We'll close the showcase with this one. It's money!"

"I know, right!" Kane says. "Pure fire!"

The studio doors open and both Franchesca and Jacob enter. Carson and Kane give them a nod and return their focus to the music. They listen as a group to the final choruses.

Everyone is nodding their heads to the music. The song eventually ends it.

"That is a single right there!" Jacob shouts excitedly.

"Very hot indeed," Franchesca agrees.

"Yeah," Kane says. Me and C was talking about using it as the closer for the showcase."

"Great idea," Jacob says, nodding.

"I agree," Franchesca says. "I'll lock down rehearsal space right away."

She turns to leave, but Carson stops her.

"Wait, Frankie," he says. "Meet me in my office. I've got a couple things to go over with you."

"I thought I was taking lead," Jacob says confused.

"You are," Carson replies. "It's about Marissa."

There is an uncomfortable silence. Kane is oblivious to the underlying current of secrets that flowed through the room.

"Y'all all right?" he asks.

"Fine," Carson answers. "Frankie, let's go."

He practically marches out Franchesca out of the studio by her left arm. Jacob takes Carson's seat.

"C's wife sick or something?" Kane asks. "They took off with a quickness."

"No," Jacob replies. "Don't worry about it. Run that track from the top again, Kane. We've definitely got a banger here."

"No doubt."

Kane cues the track and presses the playback button on the mixing interface. The single booms through the studio's far-field monitors. Both men smile as dreams of spending their impending millions dance through their heads.

CHAPTER FORTY-FIVE

Carson and Franchesca are in his office and the mood is very tense. Franchesca is holding the list of questions that Marissa had left with Carson.

"All of these questions?" she asks.

"Yeah," Carson answers. "I'm going to do it. I need you to, as well."

"This is crazy," Franchesca says.

"What we did was crazy," Carson retorts. "I'm a married man, Frankie. We never should have gone there."

"You weren't too resistant, as I recall," Franchesca says. "In fact, if I recall correctly it was *you* who knocked on *my* door."

"Franchesca, please," he pleads. "I'm trying to save my marriage."

Franchesca looks at the list of questions again. As she reviews the questions images that answer many of them pass as erotic memories in her mind. Eventually, she looks up from the page. Carson is standing before her with a look of sadness and desperation on his face.

"Please, Frankie," he says. "I don't want there to be any more secrets."

Franchesca swallows hard in this sobering moment. With nowhere to run, the truth can be a bitter pill to swallow.

CHAPTER FORTY-SIX

When Carson arrives home from the office he is exhausted but also cautious as he enters his home. Marissa's car is in the driveway – something he wasn't expecting.

The house is quiet when walks through the door.

"Marissa!" he calls out. "Mar! You here?"

There is no answer. He goes upstairs to change his clothes and look around, but she's not up there. Looking out the bedroom window to their back garden, both the pool and patio are vacant.

Maybe she's gone for a run, he thinks.

Carson quickly changes into some workout gear. Even though he's a little tired perhaps some time on the treadmill will help release some his stress.

He jogs down the stairs, but stops short as he enters the kitchen. Marissa is in the kitchen with her headphones on. She doesn't hear Carson when comes up behind her.

"So there you are," he says, lightly tapping her shoulder.

Marissa nearly jumps out of her skin as she turns to face her husband. Carson gives her a hug and she accepts it, much to his surprise.

Marissa removes her headphones.

"You startled me," she says. "I didn't hear you come in."

"Yeah, well those headphones are definitely good for blocking the world out," Carson replies.

Marissa forces a slight smile. She wants to say more, but doesn't. Marissa turns back to her cooking. Not wanting to abandon this connection, as slight as it is, Carson leans in over her shoulder in a playful manner and watches her prepare dinner.

"What'chu makin'?" he asks in that sing-song tone that Marissa's had a weakness for since college.

It's comfortable having Carson behind her. For a moment she is back in their familiar place.

"I thought chicken marsala would be nice," she replies.

Carson leans in closer.

"Sounds delicious," he says and kisses her neck. "Can I have a taste?"

Suddenly the connection is lost. Marissa stiffens at the touch of her husband's lips and she slips away from him.

"It's not that easy, Carson," she says.

"What?" he asks, innocently. "I just want a taste."

"I know," she replies. "It's the *of what* that concerns me."

Her words sober Carson from his amorous state of mind. He looks at the floor, guilt weighing upon his shoulder and sighs heavily. Suddenly something else click in him and a flint of anger alter his pose and he approaches his wife.

"You know what? Fine! I'm an asshole," he says, angrily. "I know this Marissa. I also know that for you it's about this constant need you have to ALWAYS... BE... IN... CONTROL!"

Carson marches out of the kitchen to the living room. He retrieves the list of questions that Marissa had left out for him from his suitcase. He returns to the kitchen where Marissa is waiting. She is as nervous as he is angry about what is happening. Carson forcefully hands her the papers.

"HERE!" he shouts. "Everything you want to know. Every bloody, torrid detail! It's all there. Where we did it, how many times, what I was thinking, all the positions! You know, I was hoping that we could enjoy a nice dinner before we got into..."

Carson suddenly realizes that Marissa isn't even listening to his rant. She's frantically reading the answers to the explicit questions that she had asked. Visions of her husband's heartbreaking betrayal recklessly collide in her mind. The answers are enfeeblingly shocking and with each word she's finding it harder and harder to breath.

"Ohmigod…" she says under her breath. "Ohmigod… Ohmigod… Ohmigod…"

Marissa is almost trance like as she repeats the simple phrase with each salacious revelation. Images continue to crash through the theatre of her mind like a tragic daymare.

Carson reaches out towards his wife in a desperate attempt to reconnect; to salvage their relationship. His eyes plead for understanding.

"Mar, Baby, we don't have to do this," he says.

Marissa can't catch her breath.

"I need to sit down."

She pushes past him, hard. Carson stumbles back slightly.

"Marissa," he says, reaching for her, but she is beyond his grasp.

"Not now," she says.

Marissa walks out of the kitchen leaving Carson alone to watch over dinner.

CHAPTER FORTY-SEVEN

Marissa is on the bed in the guest room reading the answers to her questions. She mumbles along as she reads in a disjointed fashion. Her tears are unstoppable as she is haunted by the visions of her husband and best friend in romantic settings, on dates… in bed… in her bed…

Her rage is quieted as equally distracting memories of herself and Sebastian interject themself into her psyche.

197

Carson is at the door. He has been there for some time, unbeknownst to his wife. It is only when she tosses the pages aside to brush away her tears that she realizes that she is not alone.

Marissa and Carson hold each other's gaze for what seems like an eternity. Her eyes transition between sadness and rage, while his between guilt, apology and longing. As the pendulum of emotions swings silent between their emotional chasm each searches the others face for common ground.

After a while, Carson takes a hesitant step towards his wife.

"Marissa," he says softly. "I don't why I did it. I don't know where you've been. I don't know who's been sending you flowers and I don't know how we got here, but *I am so...sorry...*"

He takes another step closer.

"I… am… so… sorry," he repeats.

He takes another step closer. Tears are falling on both sides.

"I am…so… sorry," he keeps saying as he closes the physical gap between them.

"I am…so…sorry…"

Marissa's voice quakes when she finally speaks.

"I know," she barely manages to say.

Carson drops to one knee in front of his wife, tears streaming down his face and rests his head on her lap.

"I am committed to fixing us," he sobs. "I know that I was stupid. I know I don't deserve you. I'm sorry. I love you. I just – just tell me how to fix this. I will do anything… Marissa, please… how do we fix us?"

"Shhh," she says quietly as she strokes her husband's head.

Looking out the window, she knows that she too needs to confess. Her mind is conflicted as to whether or not this is the time.

The shrill sound of Marissa's mobile phone ringing jars them from this moment of connectivity.

Carson sits back on the floor, letting Marissa retrieve her phone from the bedside locker. Marissa picks up the phone and looks at the call display.

It's Sebastian.

She swallows hard as guilt wells.

"Aren't you going to answer it?" Carson asks.

Marissa is frozen by the name staring back at her. Right now, timing certainly is everything.

"Mar? Answer you phone," Carson says.

Marissa mutes the ringer and gingerly sets her mobile back onto the bedside locker. She takes a deep breath and then turns back to face her husband with a forced smile.

"No need. It'll keep," she says. "This is more important. Right?"

Marissa takes a step towards her husband and Carson jumps from the off floor to embrace her.

"I swear baby," he says. "No more secrets."

"Okay."

He holds her as if even the slightest move to let her go would mean losing her forever.

"It's just you and me," Carson says. "This right here, right now… This is all that matters. Whatever happened before this moment… it's over. It never happened. It's just you and me now. Like it always should have been."

"Okay. Okay…"

Carson steps back to hold Marissa at an arms-length, staring into her eyes. His eyes take in her beauty. In this moment he can't even fathom how he could have even thought to risk throwing this away.

"I love you so much," he says.

Marissa struggle to hide her guilt and leans into the reaffirmed security of Carson's immaculately sculpted chest.

"I love you too," she replies quietly.

They hold each other close for a few moments and begin to kiss, slowly at first – soon their passion grows.

Though silenced, her phone rings again. The name on the call display is clear…

SEBASTIAN.

CHAPTER FORTY-EIGHT

From his darkened SUV parked opposite of the Winter's home beneath a low hanging tree Sebastian watches the silhouetted romancing occurring between Carson and Marissa. His jaw is clenched as he seethes with anger.

When Sebastian makes out that Carson is removing Marissa's top in the same manner he had just a few nights prior, he can't take it anymore.

Angrily, Sebastian tries to call again. Once again, he gets the machine. He doesn't leave a message, instead throwing his mobile phone aside enraged.

"Bitch!"

CHAPTER FORTY-NINE

California will always be considered a pretty chill place to live, but this morning seems to be even more relaxing than usual.

Carson and Marissa are cuddled in the guestroom bed. They slowly stir from their sleep as the gentle sounds of the neighbourhood filter into their room.

Marissa stretches and smiles at her husband.

"Good morning," she says.

"Indeed," Carson replies.

They kiss briefly and then Marissa gently pushes her husband away.

"I've got to go."

"I love you," Carson says.

"I know…"

Marissa gets out of the bed and heads out of the room. She turns back just before leaving.

"I love you too," she says.

As she leaves Marissa's mobile buzzes on the bedside locker, indicating that she has messages. Carson picks up the phone. The display says eight missed calls.

All of them are from Sebastian.

Carson is seated at the kitchen table with the paper and a cup of coffee. Marissa's mobile is also there. He stares at it accusingly. It's as if the phone is mocking him.

Marissa enters the kitchen in a rush.

"I am so late," she says. "Babe, have you seen my…"

She notices her phone on the table.

"There it is," she says.

Marissa reaches for her phone and then stops remembering that she had left it upstairs the night before. She looks at Carson.

Something is wrong.

He knows that she knows.

"Who's Sebastian?" he asks evenly.

Marissa lets out a deep sigh. There is no getting out of this situation. The apologetic look that comes over Marissa tells Carson everything that he doesn't want to know.

He looks down at the table. Hurt.

"A bartender," she starts. "I needed someone to talk to… I was so angry and hurt when I left here that night…"

"Tell me all you did was talk," Carson says quietly.

"I have to go."

She grabs her phone.

"Marissa," Carson says sternly.

"Carson, I have to go," she says, uncomfortably.

She turns to leave, but Carson gets up to stop her.

"No," he says, holding her arm. "No running away. Not this time."

"Carson, please."

"No," his voice is firm. "That's how we got here in the first place."

His eyes search her face for a hint of understanding how important this is. Finally, she relaxes her resistance.

"Okay…"

He lets her arm go.

"Did you mean it," Marissa asks.

"What?"

"Last night," Marissa replies. "When you said, we are living from last night forward and nothing before that matters… Did you mean it?"

Carson knows he's in a proverbial corner. To renege on what he had said would only serve to re-open the still healing wounds caused by his own infidelity. A dangerous silence hangs over them for a few moments.

How much is his marriage worth to him?

Finally, Carson pulls Marissa into a gentle embrace and holds her.

"I just want us to be back on," he says. "The way we were."

Marissa takes a step back and looks into her husband's eyes.

"And if you were serious then we are," she replies. "I swear to you, we are."

They kiss briefly.

"I love you, Carson," Marissa says. "You and you alone."

"And me, you," he replies.

They kiss again.

"I've got to get to the office, babe," she says,

"Okay."

Marissa walks out of the kitchen with her things. Carson pauses for a moment and then follows her through the house. Marissa's almost out the door when he calls out to her.

"Hey, Mar…"

Marissa turns around and gives a slight smile.

"Yeah?" she replies.

"Whoever *he is*, let him know I'm the only one who'll be *listening* to you from now on…"

CHAPTER FIFTY

Marissa is sitting in her car. She takes a moment to compose herself. These last few days have been so draining for her. She had thought that this morning would truly be a fresh start, but then Carson brought up Sebastian.

She looks at her phone's call history and furiously erases all evidence of the bartender's existence. Once she is satisfied that he is no longer a part of her life Marissa checks her rearview mirror, adjust the stereo and puts the car into gear. She is about to pull out of the driveway when she looks into the rearview mirror again.

Marissa screams.

Sebastian is standing in her driveway, arms crossed, blocking her path. He look furious.

"Ohmigod!" she shrieks.

Panicked she quickly gets out of her car and confronts him.

"Sebastian, what are you doing here!?!" she demands to know. "How do you know where I live? My husband could see you!"

"Oh, yeah," Sebastian sneers. "Well, he better thank me."

"What are you talking about?" Marissa asks confused.

She looks around anxiously. Marissa can't believe this is happening right now.

"You *know* what I'm talking about," Sebastian answers.

"You're crazy," Marissa says through clenched teeth.

She turns to get back into her car but Sebastian grabs her.

"Don't you ever, *EVER* say I'm crazy," he seethes.

Just then a car passes by the house. Marissa recognizes it as one of her neighbours. Sebastian releases his grip as the car drives slowly by. Marissa stumbles back slightly. Sebastian stares off into the distance as he speaks. His voice is eerily calm.

"My heart skips a beat whenever I think of you, Marissa," he says. "Right now, I am not a happy man. Walking away isn't an option for me. Perhaps, if you had no other option you would see..."

He shoots her a cold look.

"You belong with me," he says.

In the next moment Sebastian takes off leaving a slightly shaken Marissa behind. Barely a breath later, the front door of her home opens and Carson comes outside with a trash bag in hand.

"Mar? Baby, what are you still doing here?" he asks.

"I thought, I had forgotten something," she says, flustered. "But, uh, I'm just leaving. I'll see you later."

Marissa quickly gets into her Mercedes and pulls out of the driveway leaving a confused Carson behind. Carson turns back towards the house. He doesn't see Sebastian step out from the shadows across the street.

Sebastian extends his arm in the direction of Carson's back and pretends to fire an imaginary gun.

CHAPTER FIFTY-ONE

Even though he tries to shake the conversation he had with Marissa this morning, something just won't let Carson let it go.

He sits at his desk contemplating his next move. A piece of paper with Sebastian's phone number stares back at him as if challenging him to make a move. Finally, having had enough, Carson snatches up the headset for his office phone.

"Time to find out who you are, kid," he says, angrily.

Carson rotates the paper so he can read it while dialing the number. It's ringing.

One ring…

Two rings…

Three rings…

"Hello?"

Carson doesn't speak. The sound of Sebastian's voice immediately sickens him; makes it real.

"Helloooo???" Sebastian says, annoyed. "Look if you're not going to say anything I'm hanging up…"

"Is this Sebastian?" Carson asks.

It pains him to even say his name.

"Yeah, who's this?"

"Carson…Carson Winters," he says flatly.

Sebastian chuckles.

"Alright, I'll play," he says. *"Carson…* and where would I know you from?"

"Actually," Carson replies. "I believe you know my wife…"

Silence…

Sebastian is pacing on the balcony of his newly renovated apartment. He's been drinking and relaxing all day. He still has no idea who he's talking with.

"Marissa," Carson says, evenly.

Her name causes Sebastian to stop short in his tracks. Immediately memories of him and Marissa together come to mind. He smiles to himself. Feeling cocky now he takes a strong swig of his Corona before speaking.

"Oh snap! Marissa's you're wife?" he laughs. "Yeah, I know her. Pretty girl, I'm surprised she gave you my number."

"She didn't."

Carson is pissed and wants Sebastian to know it.

This information is effective in sobering Sebastian. He waits a moment before speaking. His tone is short.

"What the hell you what, man?" he asks.

"How well do you know my wife?" Carson asks.

"Hanging up now…"

Carson stands enraged, slamming his fist on his desk.

"I said, how well do you *know* my wife!" Carson demands.

"Look here!" Sebastian retorts. "You called *my phone*, all right! You want to know how well I know your girl? *Ask her*! She needed someone to listen to her 'cause apparently you've been slippin'!"

Sebastian is growing more and more enraged. How dare this punk call him as if he had done something wrong.

"She's hot, dude, and I was there!" Sebastian continues. "So yeah, I listened... I listened to her all... night... long!"

Carson sinks back into his chair as Sebastian continues his rant. Carson suspects that there is an unpleasant double entendre in the bartender's meaning.

"And you know what," Sebastian seethes. "When morning came? Yeah, when morning *came* I listened to her all... over...

again! So deal with that and don't ever call me again!"

Sebastian hangs up before Carson can speak. A shell-shocked Carson hangs up the very, very slowly. He was starting to understand how his wife felt when she caught them.

Carson felt sick. He holds his head in his hands and ponders his next move.

CHAPTER FIFTY-TWO

Sebastian is pissed. He can't believe that punk had the nerve to call him. What he does and whom he does it with is his business. Nobody ever challenges him.

Not if they don't want to feel his wrath.

Sebastian walks back into his apartment and hits redial on his phone.

A very cheerful switchboard girl answers.

"Sonic Sounds Studio. How may I direct your call?"

Sebastian hangs up.

Perfect.

He grabs his car keys and takes off out the front door.

About thirty minutes later Sebastian is seated in his Escalade staring at the entrance of Sonic Sounds Studios. A framed photograph of Marissa and Carson at their wedding is on the seat next to him on top of some clothing belonging to Marissa. Clearly he has just come from an unwelcome visit at the Winter's home.

He examines the picture again and then picks up one of her blouses. He closes his eyes as if to remember their time together as he smells the fabric in an obsessively seductive manner. Breathing in the remnants of her natural scent infused with perfume sends him over the edge. He sets the blouse aside and waits.

Time passes. He tries several times to call Marissa, but only gets her voicemail. It only enrages him more to know that she is ignoring his calls. With each rejection Sebastian's mood continues to foul.

He is silently seething, rapping his fingers on the steering wheel. He appears to be waiting… Moments later, his patience pays off.

Carson walks out of the building in a confident stride. He gets into his car and peels out of the parking lot. The moment Carson hits the streets Sebastian jumps out of his truck and strides into the office building.

A pretty girl, whom Sebastian assumes is the one he spoke with earlier, sits at the front desk. She smiles when she sees him.

"Hi!" she says. "Can I help you?"

"Uh, yeah," Sebastian replies. "I'm looking for Carson Winters."

"Oh, I'm sorry," she says cheerfully. "You just missed him."

Sebastian feigns grand disappointment. He glances down at the desktop calendar and spots tonight's showcase. This was too easy.

"You're kidding me," Sebastian says. "I have been running late all day. I was supposed to talk with him about the showcase."

"Oh," she giggles. "Are you one of the sub-promoters? 'Cause Jacob is here and he can run the event down to you."

"Oh he is?" Sebastian says. "That would be great. Thanks!"

Sebastian flashes his award-winning flirtatious smile.

"No problem," the girl says. "Just have a seat and he'll be right with you."

"Perfect."

Sebastian smiles again as he takes a seat and picks up a magazine. Hidden from the switchboard operator's view, his winning smile quickly changes to a more sinister smirk.

The hour of revenge would be upon them soon.

CHAPTER FIFTY-THREE

The Hi-fi Room has always been one of Hollywood's premiere nightspots and tonight is no different. Even though it is still early in the evening, a crowd is already gathering at the door for tonight's showcase.

Various media outlets have placed their top reporters and camera crews along the red carpet. Celebrities are also beginning to make their way along the step and repeat, pausing to pose for pictures and give interviews along their way. Hollywood has come out to play.

Sebastian is dressed to fit in with the scene. He takes out his security pass and hangs it around his neck. With a couple quick flashes of the pass he soon finds himself being let into the venue.

"Cake," he says to himself with a sly smile.

Meanwhile, Marissa and Carson are seated next to one another in the back of their hired limo as it creeps through Hollywood traffic towards Hi-fi Lounge. Carson seems nervous while Marissa is the portrait of confidence.

Sensing her husband's apprehension she takes his hand.

"You'll be fine," she says.

"I just don't want anything to go wrong," he replies.

Marissa smiles.

"You get like this before every showcase and then it goes smoother than perfection," she says. "All this stress really isn't good for you."

She turns to look out the window to watch traffic as they drive. Soon it is she who appears to be more than a little distracted. She barely hears Carson when he talks.

"This time feels different," he says. "This is the beginning of a whole new chapter... on so many levels."

An extended moment of silence passes between them.

"I don't deserve you," he says quietly.

"And yet we swore 'til death do us part," Marissa replies. "So I guess we're stuck with one another."

Carson gives his wife's hand a gentle squeeze.

CHAPTER FIFTY-THREE

A few minutes later the Winter's limousine pulls up in front of Hi-fi Lounge. The red carpet is in full swing. This makes Carson smile.

The driver opens their door and the couple step from the limo to join the media line.

As Carson and Marissa walks the red carpet, the perfect picture of Hollywood royalty, a cagey figure steps out from the shadows to observe.

It's Sebastian. He seethes with muted rage as the lovely couple pose for the world's cameras.

Sebastian shakes it off, adjusts the gun in his waistband and slips back into the club, flashing his All-Access pass.

Inside Hi-fi the night is in full swing. The opening act, an all-female R&B group is throwing down on the stage. Various entertainment reporters and industry moguls are scattered throughout the space. Fans are dancing. Everyone seems to having a great time.

Marissa and Carson are seated at their VIP table. Occasionally, Marissa looks around the room. It's a barely masked tense energy. Carson is refilling his wife's glass with Cristal when Jacob and Franchesca come over.

There is a slight tension between the two ladies as they exchange a look, but Marissa promptly masks it with a phony hospitable grin.

"Jacob, Frankie!" she says. "We were wondering where you two had disappeared to."

"Yeah, well, we'll tell you about that later," Jacobs answers, looking around the room. "Things are looking good."

Jacob pulls out a chair for Franchesca to sit down and rests his hand on her shoulder a moment longer than a friend but not long enough to be immediately confused as a lover.

Marissa catches it and shakes her head in disbelief.

"That was fast," she says under her breath.

Franchesca pretends not to hear her.

"So," Carson pipes up. "How do you want to handle the intro?"

"Frankie?" Jacob asks.

"Huh?"

"Do you want to do it with me?" Jacob asks.

Marissa chuckles to herself.

"Like she hasn't already," she says to herself.

"What'd you say, babe?" Carson asks.

"Huh, oh nothing," Marissa replies, dryly. "I think the two of them should… do it."

"I agree," Carson says.

"Me too," Jacob adds.

Franchesca scans the room and swallows hard. Her gaze lands on Marissa who silently challenges her.

"Well, there it is," Franchesca barely manages to say. "Excuse me, please."

She quickly gets up and heads towards the ladies room.

"You know what? That's a good idea," Marissa says. "Excuse me darling."

Marissa and Carson exchange a quick couple of kisses before she gets up from the table and follows after Franchesca.

Once Marissa is out of earshot Jacob turns to Carson with an approving smile.

"Things look good between you too," he says.

"Yeah, I'm a lucky man," Carson replies. "I'm real lucky."

"Me too bro'," Jacob says. "Me too."

Carson raises an eyebrow in disbelief.

"Oh, yeah?" Carson asks. "Who?"

The guys look out into the crowd to survey the scene. Unbeknownst to them there is one guest in the house that isn't exactly interested in the action on stage. Hauntingly, Sebastian appears a few steps behind the ladies, but then disappears again amidst the crowd.

CHAPTER FIFTY-FOUR

Franchesca slips into the ladies room just before Marissa catches up with her. Marissa is about to reach for the door when a hand comes out of nowhere and grabs her arm.

It's Sebastian. Marissa shrieks.

"Well, now that doesn't look like happy to see me," he says.

It takes Marissa a moment to readjust her inner compass.

"Sebastian, what are you doing here?!?"

Marissa pulls him around another corner to shield them from being seen. Sebastian laughs.

"Oh, so now you want to be alone," he says. "Well, I like what we do when we're alone."

Sebastian playfully, but aggressively reaches for her breasts. Marissa swats his hands away.

"I told you to leave me alone," she spits at him.

Sebastian leans in closer. He puts his hands against the wall, on either side of Marissa, trapping her.

"And I told you that I could *never do that…*"

Marissa desperately looks around for a means of escape. Fear begins to set in as she comes to realize the disturbing truth of what is happening. If Sebastian really wanted to hurt her no one would see them and no one would hear her screams.

"Sebastian, please," she begs. "I told you…"

"Forget what you told me," he interjects. "Let's talk about what we agreed. Let's talk about how it felt when I was deep inside you and you were begging me not to stop!"

Sebastian's eyes grow progressively more crazed as he rants.

"In fact," he seethes, "let's go talk about that with your husband. Did he tell you that he called me? Hmm? That idiot called me up and didn't even exercise a basic sense of decency!"

Marissa feels a panic attack coming on.

"No thank you or nothing. After all I did… All… night… long… Listening… How rude is that? Hmmm? You know what!?!"

238

Marissa shook her head in fear.

"I'll tell you," Sebastian says. "I think it's time Carson puts a face to name and my voice! C'mon!"

Sebastian grabs Marissa's arm forcefully and begins walk her back towards the club's main room, against her will. Suddenly, Franchesca emerges from the restrooms, startling all of them.

"Marissa?" she says, both shocked and confused.

She looks past Marissa at Sebastian and then at the grip he has on her.

"Hello," she says. "Do I know you?"

He drops his grip.

"I don't think so," Sebastian says, flatly.

Marissa steps away slightly. Franchesca is not convinced. Sebastian looks too familiar to her.

"Yes, I do," she says. "I know you... You were at the office today... You're one of the sub-promoters."

"Oh, right," he replies, his impatience growing.

"What was your name again?" Franchesca asks.

"Sebastian," Marissa offers. "He said there was a problem out front and was going to show me, but now that you're here perhaps it'd be best that he went with you. I still have to go to the restroom."

Sebastian begins to protest and grabs Marissa's arm again as she tries to step away. Franchesca knows something is up, and that there's more to this story, but won't push it. The fact that Marissa is in a roundabout way asking for her help was huge.

"Sure," she says. "Follow me, Sebastian."

Marissa breaks his grip and slips into the ladies room, leaving Franchesca and Sebastian alone. He stares at the ladies room door, angry.

"Shall we?" Franchesca prompts.

"Huh? Oh yeah," Sebastian grunts. "After you."

"No please," Franchesca insists. "After you..."

Franchesca watches with distrust as Sebastian moves past her into the main room. She follows after him. Something is off with this guy. She's sure she knows him from somewhere else. He picks up his pace and purposely loses Franchesca in a crowd of passing party revelers. When the fuss settles Sebastian is gone.

Marissa can't believe this is happening to her. As she stands in front of the sink, she knows that she can't hide in the ladies room all night.

She can't believe Sebastian went to the label.

What is his deal? Why can't he deal? Why hadn't Carson told her that he had spoken to him?

So many questions flood Marissa's mind. She feels light-headed and grabs the sinks edge to steady herself. Marissa takes a deep breath and slowly exhales. When she is feeling calmer she splashes a little cool water on her face, washes her hands and takes another brief moment to regain her poise.

The door to the ladies room suddenly bursts open. Marissa turns in fright.

A group of giggling girls stumble into the restroom. They barely notice Marissa. Clearly, they are enjoying the music and open bar this evening.

Marissa lets out a sigh of relief, gathers her purse and leaves.

CHAPTER FIFTY-FIVE

Simply put, there is probably nothing worse than a sociopathic obsessive man scorned. It doesn't matter that the club is jumping, that the bar is open and everyone else is having a really fantastic night. For Sebastian, this is the worst night of his life and only one thing will make it better.

Frustrated by his first attempt to reunite with his true love he fades to the background of the lounge and watches like a hawk the persons he believes are standing in his way on his path to true eternal happiness.

Carson, Franchesca and Jacob are oblivious to the fact that they are being watched right now. Their laughter and toasting of champagne only serves to heighten Sebastian's rage. If they were going to continue to be in his way Sebastian knew that there would be only one other option.

He reassuringly puts his hand on the concealed glock.

"What can't be had in life must surely be enjoyed in death," he says to himself.

Sebastian scans the room for Marissa. She should be back at the table by now. He's about to step outside to see if perhaps she slipped past when he finally sees her emerge from the restroom hallway.

He moves towards her as she makes her way through the crowd, his hand still on his weapon.

His excitement grows as he gets closer to her. He reaches out for towards her. The anticipation of finally being together is –

Just before Sebastian can grab her shoulder he gets violently bumped by a couple of rowdy guys. He shoves them back in anger.

"Hey! Watch where you going!" he shouts angrily.

Sebastian looks round, but Marissa is gone. Now he is furious. A sense of panic overcomes him as he turns around frantically seeking her out. Suddenly, Sebastian catches a glimpse of Marissa nearing her table.

"Oh, you're a slippery one, Marissa Winters," he says through clenched teeth.

After pushing through what seems like an endless crowd Marissa finally arrives at the VIP table. Carson isn't there. Marissa looks around for her husband, hoping that her fear is well hidden.

Suddenly, a heavy hand comes down upon her shoulder. Marissa jumps in fright, but sighs in relief upon seeing that it is her husband.

"Hey Mar," he says and greets her with a kiss. "We thought we had lost you."

Carson motions for his wife to sit as he pulls out her chair.

"Thanks," she says and sits.

"Yeah," Jacob shouted over the music. "Frankie was just telling us about a problem in the club?"

Marissa looks confused, but suddenly remembers what she had said earlier.

"Problem? There's no problem," she says and takes a deep swig of champagne.

"Sure, she said some dude," Jacob insisted. "What'd you say his name was?"

"Sebastian," Carson says evenly.

He puts a protective arm around his wife. Marissa looks over at Carson and then at Franchesca. Franchesca swallows hard, apologizing with her eyes.

"What did he want?" Carson asks.

"I don't know," Marissa replies. "But whatever it was I told him that I couldn't help him with it. I made it clear that what he wanted was more Franchesca's department."

While Jacob nodded, only Franchesca and Carson really know that there was a unflattering double-entendre in Marissa's remarks.

Marissa reaches under the table and takes Carson's hand. She looks at her husband and gives his hand a squeeze. He knows that look. He knows her signals.

He knows she's scared.

"You know what," he says to the group. "I feel like dancing. Mar?"

"Yeah," she says quietly. "I'd like that."

She gets up from the table with Carson. He takes her hand and leads her protectively through the crowd.

CHAPTER FIFTY-SIX

Sebastian is furious. The music, the lights and crowd seem to be a million miles away as he watches Carson and Marissa working their way to the backstage area of the lounge.

Angrily, he slams his fist against the railing; adjust the gun in his waistband and moves on from his perch to get closer.

It's now or never.

CHAPTER FIFTY-SEVEN

They are barely backstage when Marissa's tears begin to flow. Carson pulls her close in a protective embrace. He's still not sure of what's going on, but doesn't like that his wife is crying.

"What's going on, Mar?" he asks.

"I don't know, Carson," she sobs, "I swear, I didn't invite him here. Franchesca said he works for you, but I know that's not true. It can't be, right? Baby, please tell me that's not true."

She stops to wipe her tears and get some semblance of composure.

"He's got some balls," Carson says, angrily.

The fear racing in her eyes only makes him angrier.

"Did he hurt you?" he asks.

No response.

"Marissa? Did he hurt you!?"

"Yes, no, I mean," she stammers. "He came out of nowhere. I swear I didn't tell him about tonight. Frankie said he was at your office. Who hired him?"

"I don't know," he says, furiously. "But trust me, babe he's 'bout to paid in full."

Carson strokes her face. Another tear falls from her eye.

"Hey…hey," he says, wiping away her tears. "Look at me, look at me… look in my eyes."

Marissa looks up at her Carson.

"I got you," he says. "You don't have to worry about a thing. I've got you."

Carson kisses her, softly at first and then more passionately. There is a hunger in their embrace.

Unseen by the couple, Sebastian silently appears in the distance, gun in hand. He lifts the gun slowly and points it in the direction of their romantic embrace.

Sebastian removes the safety.

CHAPTER FIFTY-EIGHT

"And now for THE MAIN EVENT!!!" The intro to Kane's showcase rings out throughout the venue accompanied by the ever popular air raid siren sound effect.

The siren startles Sebastian causing him to stumble back into the shadow. His gun goes off, but is masked by the gunfire sound fx and deep bass of the music on stage.

There is another sound of something being bumped and crashing down from within the darkness. Marissa and Carson look over in the direction of the noise. Carson braces himself for a fight.

A slightly tipsy Jacob emerges from the shadows.

"There you two are," he says with a smile. "Dancing, my ass. Come on lovebirds. Don't get me wrong. I'm glad you're back on track, but it's time. The distributor reps are waiting. We should all be on stage together for this."

"Okay," Carson says.

He takes Marissa's hand.

"C'mon," he says. "You're not leaving my side."

Marissa follows her husband and Jacob through the crowd to the side of the stage. Franchesca is waiting for them. Together the four of them take the stage as Kane's dance troupe finishes their opening sequence.

The club is at a fevered pitch. The media are all in place and the cameras are ready to capture tonight's main action.

As Jacob steps forward, mic in hand, fans clamor to the front of the stage.

"Y'all having a good time?" he shouts.

The audience screams enthusiastically.

"I said... ARE Y'ALL HAVIN' A GOOD TIME TONIGHT!!!"

The crowd's response is almost deafening. Sebastian slowly moves from his hiding place.

"That's more like it!" Jacob continues. "Well, tonight we are here to welcome the newest member of the Sonic Sound Family! His mixtapes have been killing the underground competition and tonight... TONIGHT, we're going' ALL THE WAY LIVE!!!!"

The crowd is deafening as they scream with anticipation. With all eyes on the stage, Sebastian is able to subtly move through the crowd. Closer and closer – hand on the button his gun, ready to strike.

"LADIES AND GENTLEMEN, GET READY TO DANCE," Jacob says, enticingly. "GET READY TO SCREAM!"

With that the crowd erupts even further.

"GET READY TO LOSE YOUR MINDS, BECAUSE TONIGHT," Jacob continues. "TONIGHT, SONIC SOUNDS PRESENTS... THE ONE... THE ONLY... K to THA, A to THE, N to THAT EEEEEEEEEE!!!! KANE!!!!!"

Pyrotechnic flash pots explosions go off on either side of the stage. Waterfall pyrotechnics hype the crowd even further as the opening bars of Kane's first single, "Never Can Say Goodbye" plays out. The Jackson 5 chorus sample plays over the infectious hip hop beat as the stage lighting increases the level of excitement. The entire time Sebastian moves closer and closer to the front of the stage.

Carson, Marissa, Jacob and Franchesca move to the side of the stage as Kane emerges from behind his hip hop dancers. The ladies in the audience go crazy as hip hop newest eligible bachelor struts across the stage.

Suddenly, to her dismay, Marissa sees Sebastian; then she sees the gun. She screams.

"HE'S GOT A GUN!!!" she shrieks.

Before anyone can do anything about it the gun is raised and a wild eyed Sebastian is crushing the trigger.

BANG!

At the sound of the first gunshot Carson jumps in front of Marissa knocking her to the ground.

BANG!

BANG!

With each gunshot the crowd's screams change from excitement to fear as everyone dives to take cover.

BANG!

BANG!

Marissa can't stop screaming. Carson is on top of her. There is blood on her dress. There is blood on his jacket.

There is blood everywhere.

CHAPTER FIFTY-NINE

It's pure pandemonium at Hi-fi Lounge. Security and police are trying to secure the scene and restore order. They can't unload their weapons in the crowded room and even if they could no one can get a sight on the shooter. The entire situation is a mess.

Suddenly, six bold and decisive shots ring out.

BANG!

BANG!

BANG!

BANG!

BANG!

BANG!

When all is said and done the stage appears empty but for Marissa sobbing over her husband's body. Everyone else has scattered and the instrumental to Kane's song eerily plays the Jackson 5 sample over and over as the record skips.

A few moments pass after the shooting has ended. Slowly people start to rise up from their hiding spots. The only body that doesn't move is the one in the middle of the room, in front of the stage.

Sebastian is dead. Franchesca is closest to his body, holding a gun. She looks over to Marissa. They lock eyes in understanding. Marissa knows that this makes them square.

Outside, entertainment reporters are frantically submitting their stories live to air. There is a chaotic flurry of activity around the scene as an ambulance arrives and a stretcher is rushed inside. Amidst the aftermath Marissa cradles her husband in her lap, applying pressure to his gunshot wound.

Even though everyone is working urgently for Marissa, her world seems to be slowing down. Everything is happening in slow motion. Just as she seemed to be getting it back, her life seems to be slipping away.

CHAPTER SIXTY

The next day…

"In an unfortunate twist of events, what should have been a night for celebration ended in a violent expression of what can only be described as twisted fatal attraction.

Gunshots rang out over the debut performance of Sonic Sound's hip-hop recording artist Kane's single, "Never Can Say

Goodbye". The gunman, Sebastian Clarke, a local bartender posing as a promoter for last night's industry showcase, had apparently developed an unrequited infatuation with Marissa Winters, wife of Sonic Sounds CEO and founder, Carson Winters.

Following the shooting Mr. Winters was rushed to the hospital. Early reports state that he was shot in the chest. To date, details as to how and where the deceased met Mrs. Winters are still unclear.

A press release from the label thanks fans and friends for their continued prayers and thoughts of support, but asks that in the wake of this tragedy, that they be given some time to heal.

In related news, Kane's debut single, "Never Can Say Goodbye" is the number one requested and number one downloaded single this week. His album of the same name has been re-scheduled to be released this coming Tuesday.

Early estimates are that it will debut at number one."

CHAPTER SIXTY-ONE

Seven weeks later…

A far more relaxed Marissa Winters is lounging on the back porch of her family's Malibu beach front vacation home, watching the early morning surfers.

It is peaceful here.

Carson emerges from within the house; arm still in a sling from his most recent shoulder operation. He is skillfully balancing a tray of freshly squeezed orange juice.

He places it on the side table next to his wife and kisses her forehead.

"My college days as a waiter are coming in handy these days," he says with a smile.

Marissa smiles.

"Hey, you," she says.

"Hey, yourself," Carson replies. You seemed a million miles away right now."

"It's the ocean," she says. "It's always brought me peace."

Carson kisses her forehead again.

"Hmmm. It *is* nice here," he says.

Carson pours Marissa a glass and hands it to her. He pours another for himself and then takes a seat next to her on the same lounge chair.

They exchange a few quick kisses.

"Thank you," Marissa says.

They kiss again, a little longer this time.

"Thank you," he replies.

Marissa sips her juice slowly and looks off into the distance again. Carson follows her gaze. A sailboat drifts in the distance.

"You know," Carson says. "I was watching you from the kitchen."

Marissa looks over at him and smiles.

"You were?"

"Yeah," Carson says. "I can't help myself. Anyways, I got to thinking about you and me and this time that we've been spending together… reconnecting. It means a lot to me."

"To me too," Marissa says.

They kiss again.

"You know... we've been doing a lot of baby-making activities over these past few weeks, and well," Carson says slyly. "I just thought... How cool would that be? Having a junior Winters running around..."

Marissa smiles, but doesn't say anything.

"What do you think, babe?" Carson asks, his voice is full of hope. "About getting pregnant?"

She hesitates before talking.

"I think," she starts. "I know...that I love you..."

"But you're not ready..."

"I didn't say that," Marissa says.

Carson gets up and heads back towards the house. She can tell he's frustrated with her.

"It's okay," he says. "You don't have to. I just wanted you to think about it. You know... just think about it. No pressure..."

He is almost at the sliding door.

"Carson?"

He stops in his tracks, but doesn't look at her.

"Carson, hun," Marissa says. "Look at me… please…"

Slowly he turns to face her. Marissa stands up and begins to make her way over to her husband.

"I *have* been thinking about it," she says. "A lot. Lately, it's all I've been thinking about…"

"Okay…" he says slowly.

"But…we can't *get* pregnant now," she says.

Carson is beyond crushed, but she takes his hand and continues.

"Because I already am," she says with a huge grin.

Carson looks up his wife and smiles.

"Are you serious?" he asks.

Marissa can only nod her affirmation as tears of joy begin to fall. Carson pulls her into a huge hug and kisses her repeatedly.

"Oh Mar, this is wonderful news!" he shouts. "I'm going to be a daddy? I'm going to be a dad! I love you, I love you, I love you!!!"

"I love you too," Marissa says quietly.

Marissa holds her husband, but looks past him over his shoulder as a disturbing possible truth play in her eyes. The timing of it all is a little too close. Perhaps, Sebastian was right…

Maybe, you never can say goodbye…

271

Please turn this page for a
preview of

Judi Lewinson's
Finding Fame

Available in Spring 2011

CHAPTER ONE

"**J**ury's back."

Markus Kyle looked up from the newspaper that he was reading, took a deep breath and slowly exhaled. It was too soon. Too soon for those two words. Truth is, those judgment words, whichever they may be, would alter the outlook of several people's lives for day, weeks and years to come.

Markus grabbed his signature black leather jacket and the keys to his bike. He wasn't required to be at the courthouse for the verdict, but he had promised the victim that he would see

1

the case through to the very end. As Markus walked out the front of the precinct he was comforted by the coolness in the air and slightly overcast sky. It was a day like today when he and his former partner had met the rape victim…scratch that… Kelly-Lynn Baker was a *survivor*.

Markus grimaced slightly as the memories of their first encounter flooded his mind.

●●●

Blood-curdling screams could be heard even before the detectives stepped off of the elevator. Something about the mixture of crying and terror shook both men to the core. They quickly hustled down the long second floor apartment corridor towards unit 213.

"Unlucky for sure," Morgan grunted under his breath.

The uniform at the door nodded as the detectives flashed their badges.

"It's ugly in there," the young rookie said to the men.

"It's *always* ugly," Markus said, brushing past him.

Morgan followed.

Suddenly, both men stopped short. They'd seen a lot of pain and suffering over the course of their careers, but nothing...nothing could have prepared them for this.

Blood and broken glass were strewn everywhere. The apartment possessed the frighteningly unsavory appearance of death. If it weren't for the victims screaming mixed sobs there one would be hard pressed to believe that anyone had survived this.

"She fought with him," Markus said quietly as he scanned the room. "Good."

This had been an all out fights fight. Evidence showed that the struggle had begun in the living room. There was a blanket on the sofa and turned over bottle of wine on the floor near a remote.

"Looks like she was sleeping or watching the TV when the attacker came in," Morgan said.

Markus remained silent. He stroked his chin, part in anger, part in meditation. The crime scene unit was photographing the scene. With each flash came a brutally jarring image of what had happened here. His senses were overloading with the violent temperament of it all. Disgust rose like bile after a nauseating meal. The worst of it was in the bedroom. Her screaming and sobbing was beyond deafening. She was terrified. She didn't want anyone to touch her.

How do you tell someone that their fear in this moment wasn't the priority? That with each moment that passed so increased the assailants chance of escaping justice?

Answer…You didn't.

Still, the crime scene unit wouldn't be able to get in to do their job until the paramedics got her out.

Markus walked to the threshold of the bedroom and silently motioned for everyone to leave. There was a brief protest, but the stern look on Markus Kyle's face made it very clear that he was not to be crossed in this moment.

Slowly, the other officers began to leave. As the room emptied, the victim's sobbing and screaming began to subside. Morgan took a couple of the officers aside for a quick briefing. Markus took a moment's pause before he entered the room. Already the energy in the room had begun to change.

Shrunken in the farthest corner of the bedroom was nineteen year old, Kelly-Lynn Baker. Already diminutive in stature, the five foot four ~~woman~~ girl, looked even smaller in this moment. Markus moved to be a few feet in front of Kelly-Lynn. Her pained cries were now more a traumatized whimper.

He sat down on the floor, cross legged, in front of her.

Then Markus waited.

Her knees were pulled close to her chest. Kelly-Lynn's hair had already begun to matte in the blood from where she had been repeatedly struck. She was shivering, but Markus knew that that was more a symptom of her calming down rather than that of being cold.

Slowly, Kelly-Lynn lifted her head. No longer an innocent, her once doe eyes spoke a silent yet hardened tale of the vicious brutality she had recently come to know.

Now he would speak.

"My name is Detective Markus Kyle and I'm going to get the man who did this to you."

●●●

Join Today!
Judi Lewinson's
Official Fanclub

Keep up to date on
upcoming releases,
contests & appearances.

www.judilew.com

WWW.JUDILEW.COM